Ratspell

I can still remember how we huddled together in the nest, my brothers and sisters and I, when my mother whispered, "Go to sleep or Scrunchy the Shoemanbeing will get you." I suppose you thought with usual human arrogance that you alone told stories to your children. We Rats have always kept our history alive by the telling of tales. We have great respect for our storytellers and a good thing too. As a very small Rat, I'd have been tail up and twisted long ago if the tribe hadn't looked on me as a Teller of Tales.

Other titles in the *Hippo Fantasy* series:

The Night of Wishes
Michael Ende

The Wednesday Wizard
Sherryl Jordan

Rowan of Rin
Emily Rodda

The Practical Princess
Jay Williams

Watch out for:

Malcolm and the Cloud-Stealer
Douglas Hill

Hippo Fantasy

Ratspell

Paddy Mounter

Hippo

Scholastic Children's Books,
Scholastic Publications Ltd,
7–9 Pratt Street, London NW1 0AE, UK

Scholastic Inc.,
555 Broadway, New York, NY 10012-3999, USA

Scholastic Canada Ltd,
123 Newkirk Road, Richmond Hill,
Ontario, Canada L4C 3G5

Ashton Scholastic Pty Ltd,
P O Box 579, Gosford, New South Wales,
Australia

Ashton Scholastic Ltd,
Private Bag 94407, Greenmount, Auckland,
New Zealand

First published in hardback by Scholastic Publications Ltd, 1993
First published in paperback by Scholastic Publications Ltd, 1994

Text and illustrations copyright © Paddy Mounter, 1993

ISBN 0 590 55462 X

Typeset by TW Typesetting, Midsomer Norton, Avon
Printed by Cox & Wyman Ltd, Reading, Berks.

10 9 8 7 6 5 4 3 2 1

Contents

~PART TWO~
THE RAT'S TALE

An Introduction by the Author

It's early morning. I am sitting at the front of an old wooden barge drifting down a green tunnel of leaves. Patches of sunlight glide towards me on the black water and scatter to bright fragments under the bows. The air is full of bird song. I can hear – I have very sharp ears – the putt, putt, putt of the barge's engine and the soft slap of water on the hull. I can smell old wood, tar, diesel oil, cheese and onion crisps and frying bacon mixed with the million smells that a breeze from the open country-side brings to a traveller with a keen sense of everything. This has been my life for a very short time – but I know that there's nowhere in the wide world I'd rather be.

The barge is the home of my good friend and travelling companion Miss Jezabella Jones, the actress. For more years than anyone can remember she has chugged the length and breadth of the country, as much a legend on the canals as she is in the theatre. If you were ever brave enough to ask why she chose to travel in such a slow and inconvenient way, she would draw herself up to her full height (about two metres), pin you to the wall with eyes like laser beams and tell you in a voice that could crack a coconut at fifty paces, "I detest trains, can't abide the autobus and would not be seen dead in one of those smelly little automobiles. I travel by barge and if a theatre doesn't have sense enough to be built near a canal, my dear, then it doesn't get Miss Jones."

At the moment, Miss Jones is sitting at the other end of the barge, steering with one hand

and frying with the other. On her head is a hat like an untidy roof garden. She is wearing a huge, flowery dressing gown – given to her, she says, by Kumquat of the north, a red-headed Eskimo wrestler from Stockton-on-Tees – odd football socks – one Liverpool, one Everton – and Doc Marten boots. ("Physicians to the feet, my dear, and wonderfully comfortable.") She is as bright and colourful as her own painted barge and every day that passes I thank my lucky stars that my adventures landed me on her deck. There is more to tell of Miss Jones, but that comes much later in my tale.

Before you read any further there is something I think you ought to know. Don't think for one moment I'm confessing to something I'm ashamed of, I'm rather proud of it as a matter of fact. You may have wondered why I am lounging about in the sunshine and not lending my friend a hand. Well, the fact is I haven't got any hands to lend – I've got paws. I've got sticky-out teeth, small pink ears and a long scaly tail. My name is Spratt and I'm a Rat, a very small Rat maybe but a member of the great tribe *Rattus rattus* none the less and therefore, by the nature of the world – your enemy.

Of course, it's just possible that you're not afraid of Rats. You may have met one of my domesticated cousins and know what an excellent companion a Rat can be. If so, my friend, you are the exception. For centuries your fables have been riddled with the evil Rat. We burrow through your legends. We scuttle through your nightmares and yet we have never intentionally done you any harm. How much more have we to fear from you? Wouldn't you be afraid of something as tall as a ten-storey building, with stamping feet, big as double-decker buses? With arms that throw and swing sticks the size of trees? No wonder we hide, skulk in dark corners and run from you in terror. No wonder that our myths are peopled with long-armed giants, crunching boots and snarling traps.

I can still remember how we huddled together in the nest, my brothers and sisters and I, when my mother whispered, "Go to sleep or Scrunchy the Shoemanbeing will get you." I suppose you thought with usual human arrogance that you alone told stories to your children. We Rats have always kept our history alive by the telling of tales. We have great respect for our storytellers and a good thing too. As a very small Rat, I'd have been tail up and twisted long ago if the tribe hadn't looked on me as a Teller of Tales.

My mother says I began telling stories in the nest. I don't remember but I know that after my accident with the mackerel tin, of which I shall tell you later, I'd say anything that came into my head to stop the scratching and biting of my larger sisters and brothers. Sometimes it worked and they stopped and listened, so I suppose I had some natural talent. But it wasn't until Uncle Sharkie asked me to become his apprentice, much to the surprise of the whole tribe, that I really learnt the art. Uncle Sharkie was surely the greatest storyteller in the whole history of Rattery. He could weave spells with words of such magic that the oldest, dustiest tale would sprout wings and fly.

"You must never forget, little Spratt," he would say, "all the wisdom and cunning that has helped our tribe survive is wrapped up in our tales."

And survive we have. Whether you like it or not we have shared your homes and your history for a thousand years and more. Hidden behind the walls of cottages and castles, we listened to the gossip of ploughmen and the whispered secrets of kings and wove them into tales to pass down the centuries.

So if you'd like to hang on to this Rat's tale,

we'll follow the fate of my tribe and the Big-noses, a family of your tribe. We'll scuttle down the twists and turns of history and you'll hear how closely our tales have intertwined.

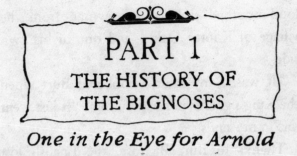

PART 1
THE HISTORY OF THE BIGNOSES

One in the Eye for Arnold

"Oh, Rats!" said Arnold, King of England. "Here comes the naffin' rain." His Majesty lifted his visor and squinted up at the sky. The battle bashed and clashed around him.

"Hold up! . . . What's this then?" he rubbed the rain from his eyes. "Oh conkers! It's an . . . Ahhhhhhhhh!!" These were His Royal Majesty's last words before an arrow hit him in the eye, but you won't find those words in your history books. Your history didn't think they were kingly enough to be written down. Your history says he was shot by a French archer.

That's not true either. I know for a fact he was shot by Burt Bignose, a drunken, thieving, loud-mouthed slob of a bowman from the village of Knotty Oak – and one of his own side.

"It wasn't my fault," slobbered Burt when the King's guards jumped on him. "It just went 'orf in me 'ands."

Thanks to Burt Bignose, the English lost their king and soon after, lost the battle.

When the victorious French rounded up their prisoners, they couldn't understand why Burt was already in chains.

"I were on your side all along," lied Burt. "With one shot of my trusty bow, I, Burt Bignose of Knotty Oak, did wondrous bravely lay low the villainous King Arnold and won the battle for our rightful King Norman of France. I, Burt Bignose of Knotty Oak, did single-handed . . ."

"Shuddup your fat face," snarled his guards. "Keep your story until you stand before ze

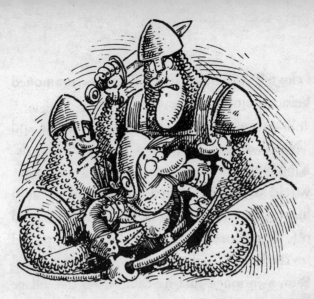

great King Norman. Who knows, it may even make him smile as he chops off your fat head."

After the battle, the great King Norman, who now called himself "Norman the Conqueror", set off on a grand tour of his new kingdom to chop off some heads and count his winnings. Burt was thrown into a Rat-infested dungeon. This always seemed to me to be very unfair to the Rats. How would you like a fat, smelly bowman squatting in your living-room for a year and more? It was a great relief to the Rats,

I can tell you, when at last Burt was summoned before the new king and his court.

With many "Yes, Your gurt Majesty"s and "No, Your gurt Majesty"s, Burt told his tale. King Norman had already decided what history would say. All he wanted was for Burt to finish his story quickly so that he could chop his head off. King Norman stared at the ceiling, picked his teeth with his dagger and looked bored until Burt mentioned that he came from the village of Knotty Oak. The king sat up.

"Knotty Oak! Knotty Oak! Did ze prisoner say Knotty Oak?"

The clerk to the court cleared his throat.

"Ahem! . . . Er yes, My Liege. I believe the prisoner did allude to a settlement of that appellation."

King Norman jumped to his feet and crossed the hall to a book, bound in leather and iron, marked in fresh gold paint GLOOMSDAY BOOK. This great book was his pride and joy. In it his Inspectors had listed every town and

village, every serf and servant, pig, cow and plough in his new kingdom. The king loved money, and with a tax on everything he would become very, very rich. With some effort he threw back the cover and began leafing through the Ks.

"Knatty! ... Knetty! ... Knitty! Yes! Knotty Oak, I knew zat ze name clanged a bell." At the top of the page, in large letters, were the words INSUFFICIENT INFORMATION. At the bottom, pinned to one corner, was a note. I can tell you exactly what it said, because an ancestor of mine was unlucky enough to get himself locked in a chest with a copy of the GLOOMSDAY BOOK. He ate his way from F to K before he managed to escape.

Report to Norm. Conc. Re. Knotty Oak

Initial inspection showed the village to be of unusual aspect as it stands within an ancient circle of stone (poss. Gurrassic Limestone). This great stone circle is much revered by the villagers. Further inspection revealed a natural spring known as Nickspiddle Spring, that rises from the roots of a hollow oak (*Quercus rober*) at the very centre of the village. When my superior, the Chief Inspector of Villages, demanded information in the name of King Norman, the villagers became abusive. They called upon the occupant of the hollow oak (one Nell the Spell), who told my superior to 'hop it' and changed him into a small green frog (*Rana temporaria temporaria*). The Chief Inspector was chased into the spring by Ms Spell's cat, at which point I terminated the survey.

Pierre Le Drain (Assistant Inspector of Villages)

The king slammed the great book with a bang that echoed all around the hall.

"How dare zese peasants make frogs of my Inspectors!" He paced up and down. "How dare zey spoil my book with zis 'insufficient information'." He spat the words out like sour lemons.

"Zey must be made to pay." He stopped pacing and stared thoughtfully at the cringing Burt. Then an awful thing happened, something no one at court had ever seen before. Slowly, very slowly, the king's lips parted and . . . he smiled. A smile that was like the opening of a grave. He reached up, took a huge sword from the wall and strode to the centre of the hall. "Come here, you snivelling worm."

Burt snivelled and clanked his way towards the king.

"By what name are you called?"

"B . . . B . . . Burt . . . B . . . B . . . Bignose, if it please Your gurt Majesty." Slowly the king raised the huge sword above his head. Down it came. There was a gasp from the court. Bert jumped a metre as the blade touched him lightly on the shoulder.

"Arise, Sir Burt Bignose." Burt didn't move. He stared at the king and blinked. Norman the Conqueror kicked him impatiently. "Get up, you fat pig. I 'ave just made you Lord of ze Manor of Knotty Oak."

I've always had a sneaking admiration for King Norman. We Rats have a great respect for cunning and his plan was both cunning and simple. Was there a better man to collect taxes than one who had spent most of his life robbing his neighbours? Burt knew the owner of every pig, pot and plough in Knotty Oak, and, as Sir Burt Bignose, his spiteful greed would make the villagers' lives a misery. No wonder the king smiled. He would get his taxes and his revenge. As for Burt, he couldn't believe his luck.

"I shall make 'em pay, all right," he gloated, "and they'll curse the very day they drove Burt Bignose out of 'ouse and 'ome."

A Horrible Knight

The news that Burt Bignose was to return as Lord of Knotty Oak spread through the village like the plague. A black cloud of gloom hung over the villagers gathered in Widow Woodbine's ale house. Ned the Bread sat in a corner wringing his floury hands.

"There's nothing to be done," he moaned. "We're as dead as dumplings."

"Aye," agreed his neighbour. "I'd as soon serve under the Devil himself as under a Bignose."

Ned stared into his ale. "Perhaps we hadn't

ort to have called on Nell the Spell to rid us of the varmint in the first place."

"Nonsense, ye great loaf," snapped his wife. "You know as well as I it had to be done. There's never been a Bignose yet as was half as useful as a dead ferret, and Burt's the worst of the lot." She looked around at her neighbours. "There's not one among us as hasn't suffered by his wickedness. The pity of it is that he took hisself off before Nell got to work on him. Why, you know yourselves his poor wife and family were gladder than any to see the back of him."

"Well, word is that tomorrow will see the front of him again – and his horrible gurt nose," wailed Ned, "and I for one hope never to see a worser day!"

The village seemed as quiet as the grave, just a few scrawny chickens pecking in the dust by the spring. Burt wasn't fooled. He'd seen the sacks in the windows twitch as they rode by. The new Lord and his troop of French soldiers

pulled up at the edge of the green.

"Get 'em all out!" he commanded. "Beat down their doors if you have to. I want every man, woman and child, dog, pig, chicken and Rat to know that I, Sir Burt Bignose, be their new lord and master." It was soon done. Burt looked down on his former neighbours.

"Thought you got rid of me, did you?" he snarled. "Well, you han't. Thought you'd be better off without me, did you? Well, you ain't, because by order of His gurt Majesty, King Norman the Conqueror, all that was yours is mine and you are to be my serfs and slaves. What do ye think about that?"

The villagers didn't dare say what they thought. They stared sullenly at the ground while their new lord ranted on and on about the way they had mistreated him in the past.

His Lordship didn't notice a crow that flapped from a nest in the great oak. He didn't notice it circle and hover above his head. He did notice when something landed with a plop on his new French hat. His Lordship stopped in mid-rant. He took off his hat and stared at it, then at the oak whence the message came. The meaning was clear enough – he wasn't the lord and master of Nell the Spell.

The winter that followed is said by our Storytellers to have been the hardest that ever was. If the villagers had little, the Rats had less and only the strongest survived. From cockcrow to the last rook to roost, the village rang to the sound of pick and shovel on the iron-hard earth as the villagers slaved to build a manor house for their new lord. They grew thin in the bitter cold while Burt and his household kept fat and warm. By the time Sir Burt proclaimed the first of May to be his housewarming day, the villagers were all but starving.

"Summat's got to be done, neighbours," announced Ned the Bread, "or there's not a soul among us will live to see the sun rise over the Summer-stone. Saturday night, we'll meet at the Bakehouse. Burt and his men will be carrying on at Widow Woodbine's ale house, so we should be safe enough."

By ten on Saturday, the little bakery was packed as tight as a bull in a bread bin. Ned stood on an empty flour barrel. He coughed importantly and called for quiet.

"Well, neighbours," he began, "summat's got to be done . . ."

"Yes, so you keep saying," interrupted his wife, "but what can we do against old Pignose and his gurt bundle of soldiers? Hark at 'em!" She waved an arm in the direction of the noise from the ale house. "Drinking and cursing and singing their rude Frenchy songs . . ."

"It's that poor wife of his that I feel sorry for," chimed in Fermity Hogswallow. "All those smelly soldiers' socks to wash, and have you heard the latest? He says he wants to change his name to Sir Ethelburt Le Nez, and she has to mark it in gold thread on all his clothes."

"Apart from his hat," said someone. "That's been marked already."

"Neighbours! Neighbours!" shouted Ned above the laughter. "We didn't come here to gossip. Gossiping won't get rid of the varmints. Doesn't anyone know where we can turn for help?"

It was old Mother Toadflax who finally

spoke up and put words to the thoughts of them all.

"We must do as we did before," she croaked. "We must seek the help of Nell the Spell."

You Could Never Tell with Nell

Throughout the winter, Nell and her cat had watched the building of the manor house, perched in the crow's nest at the top of the oak tree. Burt knew she was watching him but didn't know what to make of it. You never knew with Nell. A farmer might ask her for something to get rid of the Rats in his barn. The Rats might send a deputation to ask her to rid them of the farmer. It was heads or tails whether Rats or farmer disappeared.

Nell was unpredictable – even dangerous. Quite a number of my ancestors living in the roots of the great Oak ended their days as an ingredient in one of her brews, so I can understand why the villagers were reluctant to ask her for help.

Oh yes, Nell was unpredictable all right. Her hair, for one thing. It was usually bright red and sprang from under her hat with a life of its own. But on her bad days, it would turn black and as spiky as daggers. And her eyes! It was best not to look into her eyes, but a quick glance would tell you that one was sea green, the other sky blue. Most of the time, Nell did the sort of things you'd expect of a village witch – weaving love charms, boiling newts, getting rid of (or giving people) warts and boils. Then, without warning, she'd decide to be a porcupine for a week, or a crocodile or even a porcudile and splash about in the spring, frightening the children. Much worse were the black thunder rumble days, when she would crouch over her stone and call up the spirit of an older, wilder world. The Great Oak would tremble. The

spring would froth and boil and the villagers would crawl under their beds and hide. No, you could never tell with Nell the Spell.

At midnight, after the meeting in the bake-house, a small group of villagers huddled before the Great Oak.

"Who's going to pull it, then?"

"You can. You're the oldest."

"Lizzie Turnip! Everyone knows that you've seen a sackful more summers than I. Ned, you're the tallest. You pull it."

"I can't. Me arms hurted with the rheumatiz. Why don't we . . ."

"Oh, get out of my way," hissed Ned's wife. "Else we'll be here till dawn." She barged past and pulled hard on the rope.

"Ding dong!" cawed a crow from somewhere above them, and the door in the Oak creaked open. There stood Nell the Spell, wearing a party hat. The cat wore a flashing green nose. By the light of the nose the villagers could see that Nell was holding a large cracker and a cake.

"Presents for His Lordship's housewarming," she sang, thrust the bundle at Ned's wife and disappeared inside the tree with a slam. They all stared at the cake.

"Lord love us!" whispered Ned's wife. "'Tis a likeness of the Manor House down to the very last stick."

The cake caused a lot of argument. The villagers didn't like the idea of giving Burt anything, but what could they do? It didn't pay to cross Nell the Spell. They decided to leave the presents on the doorstep for Lady Bignose to find in the morning.

"Wash thish then?" spluttered His Lordship through his breakfast porridge. His wife plonked the presents onto the table in front of him.

"I think it's something the villagers left, dear."

"Where would they get such things as these?"

"I really don't know, dear. Be careful, dear, it might be poisoned."

"Ha!" said Burt. "That lot wouldn't dare." He poked the sugary thatch with a grimy finger. "Hmmm. It tastes good enough. They'll be wanting an invite to my housewarming, that's what. Well, let 'em want. I'll not have that bunch of peasants past *my* doorpost."

Now, here is something that has always puzzled me. Rats will either like or dislike one another depending on their nature. It doesn't seem to be the same for human beings. No sooner had Burt become Sir Burt, than important folk from the villages all around, who would have choked rather than give the time of day to the bad old Burt, were falling over each other for an invitation to Sir Burt's housewarming party.

By early evening on the first of May, Knotty Oak Manor House was packed. At first the party went well enough. The guests admired the cake and Burt, full of ale and as merry as a mangel-wurzel, decided to pull the cracker with himself. It went with a bang and they all cheered. Out fell a rolled-up paper crown, a candle in a spiked holder and a small card. Burt put on the crown and picked up the card.

"Warmest wishes from all." He threw it aside. "Bah! A plague on their warm wishes! Bring me a light for the candle!" As he drove the spiked candle into the roof of the cake, there came a great creaking groan from above. Some of the guests looked up in fright as straw and splinters fell around them.

"Wassamatter with you lot?" snarled Burt. "Just the new roof timbers settling. Where's that light?" Someone handed him a stick from the fire. He lit the candle, sat back in the glow and beamed at his cake, then he took a huge breath, leant forward and blew with all his might. The candle flickered and grew brighter. How the crowd laughed and jeered. Another huge breath and the Lord of Knotty Oak blew till his eyes popped and the candle grew brighter still. The more he blew the higher rose the flame. Crackling sparks shot towards the thatch. Coloured stars popped and zoomed around the hall.

"Put it out! Put it out, it's bewitched!" screamed His Lordship. He emptied his ale over the cake. 'Twould have been as well to douse the flames with petrol. Woomph! Liquid fire snaked among the dishes of the feast-laden table. It ran across the floor. It singed Burt's nose and set afire his paper crown. In panic he brought his mug down on the roof of the flaming cake. Crash!! At the same instant, something huge smashed through the roof of the new Manor House. Thatch and timber rained down as the Lord and his guests fought and scrambled their way towards the door.

They escaped with a few burns and bruises. Burt, black with soot and purple with rage, ordered the villagers out of their houses. A chain of buckets from the spring made little difference. By morning, Knotty Oak Manor was burned to the ground.

For two days Burt ranted and raged around the smouldering ruin. How his bandaged nose throbbed! How his singed head ached! How was he going to think of something terrible enough to punish the villagers? He wanted to chop them into little pieces, feed them to the Kites, throw them to the Buzzards. But that wouldn't do. Who then would work in his manor? Who would rebuild his house? He was sitting on a charred beam staring at the ashes when a messenger arrived on horseback, dusty from a long ride. It was Pierre le Drain.

"Do I have the honour of addressing the Lord of Knotty Oak?"

"Who wants to know?"

"My name, my Lord, is Pierre le Drain. I am

the bearer of orders from His Majesty King Norman the Conqueror."

"Well, give 'em 'ere and shove off," snarled Burt. Pierre stood his ground.

"You fail to comprehend the significance of my presence, my Lord. I am commanded by His Majesty to remain in this locality for a period not less than that which it takes to complete the project referred to herein."

With a flourish, he thrust a large scroll under Burt's nose.

"I fail to comprehend you at all," snarled His Lordship. He snatched the scroll and broke the seal.

As he read, his nose stopped hurting and his headache disappeared. He threw the scroll in the air.

"The King be praised!" he shouted. "Thank you, oh gurt and wonderful King Norman."

The King had ordered Burt to build a castle at Knotty Oak. As I've told you before, King Norman was no fool. He sent Pierre le Drain to keep an eye on Burt until the castle was finished.

His Lordship was as merry as a mouse in a mill, for the castle had solved his problem.

"You need lots of stone to build a castle. I'll make 'em smash up their precious stone circle. You need lots of water for a moat, so I'll take their piddling little spring and for the roof timbers – I'll chop down that dratted 'gurt oak'.

That'll teach 'em or my name's not Burt . . . er, I mean Ethelburt Le Nez."

Burt was a happy man and the more the villagers begged and pleaded for him to change his mind, the happier he became.

By Oak and Spring and Devil's Horn

The king's builders arrived and the great stones that had circled Knotty Oak for thousands of years were all thrown down in a day. As each stone fell, a rumbling groan deep in the earth shook the village to its roots. Nickspiddle Spring hissed and boiled like a witch's cauldron and a sulphurous mist bubbled from its waters, catching the throat, stinging the eyes. It coiled around the village like a yellow snake, under the doors of the terrified villagers, creeping right down into the very Ratholes of my ancestors.

I remember how Uncle Sharkie's eyes would blaze whenever he told the tale of the felling of the stones.

"It stirred up old gods, little Spratt, and as sure as fate it meant a dance with the Devil for the Lord of Knotty Oak."

During all this to-do, Nell the Spell shut herself away in the Great Oak. The villagers were afraid to go near her and I can't say I blame them. By the time the last stone lay in pieces, Burt was feeling pretty pleased with himself. He sat in his favourite chair while his wife pulled off his boots.

"Well, wife," he said, "I've taken their stones for me castle, I've diverted their spring for the moat and still not a peep out of that meddlesome witch." He took a long swig from his ale, belched loudly and wiped his whiskers with the back of his hand. "So, tomorrow we're going to chop down the Great Oak."

His wife heaved at his boot.

"Do you think that's wise, dear?" she panted.

"Don't forget the trouble you had with the cake."

"Nothing but fiddling fireworks and sugary pokery," shouted Burt. "Do you think that I, Sir Ethelbert le Nez, are just a wart to be charmed away by some rag-bag village witch?" He banged the table with his fist.

"I be Lord of Knotty Oak and I say that tomorrow that tree shall be felled."

Just after dawn the next day, soldiers could be seen marching across the green to the great Oak. They were surprised to find Nell sitting in the crow's nest. They shouted at her to come down. "We 'ave orders from his Lordship to chop down zis tree." Nell refused to move.

"Chop away, me hearties," she called. "You look like you could do with the exercise, but you won't get so much as a matchstick for His fat Pigship."

The soldiers marched up to the tree, watched by a ring of silent villagers. They rolled up their

sleeves, spat on their hands and swung their sharp and shiny axes.

Thunk! Thunk! Thunk! The blades bit deep into the tree . . . and stayed there. More axes were sent for and they too stuck fast. The soldiers attacked the tree with saws, chisels, knives and swords. Everything stuck fast, until the old Oak bristled like a hedgehog.

"Just the job to hang me washing on," jeered Nell. Red-faced and exhausted, the soldiers eventually gave up and marched away to the cheers of the villagers.

There was little else for the villagers to cheer at as they sweated and slaved to build the new castle. As for the Rats, it was only Burt's wickedness that saved them from starvation. While the villagers picked and shovelled deep into the earth, my ancestors toiled alongside them, digging passages of their own. It was hard but it was worth it, for no sooner were the dungeons finished, than Burt began to fill them with corn stolen from his neighbours. As the castle rose stone by stone, so the Rats tunnelled deep inside the walls and grew fat on the stolen corn. Even before the last stone was laid, Knotty Oak Castle had been invaded and occupied by my ancestors.

I expect you've seen a castle or two, soft crumbling ruins most of them, sticking up through bowling-green grass. The new castle at Knotty Oak wasn't like that. It was hard-edged and dangerous, bright and sharp-chiselled for war. King Norman the Conqueror was reminding his people who was boss.

It was two years later that Burt stood on his new battlements and looked out across his land. In the time of the castle building, his wickedness and greed had made him a rich man. Now he could afford to spend a little and show off to his neighbours.

"Better get thyself a new frock," he said to

his wife. "Nothing too fancy, mind. We're going to hold a tournament at Midsummer Fair and there'll be a banquet on the green for the better folk. I've told that nosy parker Pierre le Drain to make himself useful for once and order the food. None of they French muck, I told him. We'll have Swan in t' Basket – although come to think of it, Boar's Head in t' Bucket might be cheaper. I'll make a speech and the drawbridge will be ceremonially lowered."

"Very nice, dear. You decided against a castle-warming then?" Burt looked at his wife sharply. Sweetly, she smiled back.

The great day dawned to sun and clear skies. People from many miles around began arriving at first light, and by mid-morning the green blazed with colour. Flags fluttered. Bands blared. There were jugglers, jousters, pedlars, puppets and popinjays. Oxen were roasted. Sheep were slaughtered and sizzled on spits. Bears were baited. Hunting dogs fought over bones. Knights clanked and collided, denting each other with iron conkers on sticks. Teeth were knocked out. Arms were broken. Children ran and laughed among the coloured tents for the very joy and noise and smell of a medieval fair.

The Bignose Curse

When his guests had feasted, Sir Burt Bignose, full of wine and self-importance, picked his way from the banqueting table, over bones and snarling dogs, to a small stand next to the drawbridge. Unsteadily, he climbed the steps and waited for his soldiers to silence the crowd. I won't bore you with his speech. It was long and mostly about himself. When he'd finished, to a rattle of polite applause, he chopped through a ribbon with his battle axe. To the blare of trumpets the bridge began to drop at full speed. Halfway down it stopped.

Raised voices were heard from inside the castle.

"Wot you stopped winding for then?"

"Because His Lordship said wind it slow and you're winding like a mill-in-a-gale so's you can get back to your ale, piddlehead."

"Oh, ar! Well, if I weren't 'olding of this 'andle I'd show you who was a piddlehead."

"Oh, ar! Why, you . . . Ouch!!" . . . Biff! . . . Thump. . . ! There was a whirring and a dragging of chains as handles were let go to settle the argument. The heavy bridge dropped onto its stone supports with a crash that seemed to lift the whole castle from its foundations. Burt's platform collapsed and he pitched forward into a tangle of flags and broken timber. There were shouts of laughter when his head poked up through the rubble. Burt lost his temper and his dignity.

"Think it's funny, eh?" he snarled. "One more squeak out of any of ye and ye'll rot with the Rats in my dungeons."

The long silence that followed was broken by

a tinny cackle. "Hee! Hee! Hee! Hee! Hee! Hee!" It seemed to float over the crowd. "Hee! Hee! Hee! Hee! Hee! Enjoy your fortune while you may, Lord of Knotty Oak, for your time is running faster than your big blubbery nose. Fate is gnawing at your timbers, you squint-eyed stone-robber. Doom is nibbling at your bones, you pimple-headed water-snatcher . . ."

The Lord of Knotty Oak looked as if he would burst. His great nose had gone bright red. It throbbed and bristled like an angry cactus. On went the tinny voice with insults far too rude for me to tell. The crowd looked around in wonder.

"It's the spirit of the spring risen up to haunt him."

"No, it's the voice of the broken stones come back for revenge."

"'Tis a wood sprite come to punish him for his wicked ways."

Burt knew who it was.

"It's that maggoty witch, Nell the Spell."

With a roar he charged through the crowd and hit the Great Oak a mighty blow with his battle axe. Boing! The blade bounced off as if the Oak were made of rubber. His Lordship spun like a top and fell in a heap. The axes, swords and saws that had rusted into the tree began shooting out in all directions.

A voice shouted, "Look out! 'Tis falling. The old Oak is falling on His Lordship!"

Sir Burt looked up in horror. Under some power of its own, the huge tree was toppling towards him. A deep, menacing groan, a snapping of roots, the old Oak was tearing itself from the earth. Burt scrabbled backwards in the dirt.

"Ahhhhh! Get back! Get back, ye gurt murderous stump!!"

The crowd waited for the Lord of Knotty Oak to be squashed like a beetle. But not so much as the smallest twig touched his cringing Lordship, for as the old tree fell, it crumbled away to nothing. A brown cloud of dust hung in the air where the Oak had been. It drifted away on the breeze and there, sitting on her stone, was Nell the Spell with the cat perched on her head.

Burt rubbed the dust from his eyes, as if he couldn't believe what he was seeing.

"What devilry is this?" he hissed.

"For once you are right, my lumpy Lord," replied his tormentor. "So beware, for I be the guardian of the Devil's left horn."

Burt was beyond all reason. "To hell with you and the Devil!!" He rushed at her. Down came his axe but cat and witch had gone and his blade hit the stone with a bone-shaking clang! A splinter, like a small shooting star, flew up – a rumbling roar, deep underground.

"Ahhhhh! She's blinded me!" he screamed and clutched his eye. "Grab her! Bind her! Tie her up with ropes! Weigh her down with chains!"

Nervously, the soldiers did as they were ordered. Nell and the cat seemed to be quite

happy to be trussed up and weighed down.

"Drag them to the moat!" The soldiers dragged them off and the crowd followed. Burt was helped to the drawbridge. Still holding his eye, he addressed the crowd.

"Let it not be said that the Lord of Knotty Oak be an unjust man. If she floats then she's guilty and we'll burn her for a witch, as has always been the custom. If she sinks and drowns, then she's innocent . . . throw her in!"

Nell didn't float or drown. When she hit the water, she bounced – and she and the cat went on bouncing around the moat as if it were a trampoline, cackling, clanking and cursing poor old Burt:

"Ratspell, Sprattspell, Blackspellation,
Doomed to Ratelimination.
I curse thee Burt, you one-eyed Rat
(and by the way, so does the cat).
To Rattify in one short speech
Parts other curses cannot reach,
By Oak and Spring and Devil's Horn,
You'll wish that you were never born.
And you won't laugh, oh, dear me no,
When your whiskers start to grow.
And just how long do you suppose
Will grow your itchy, twitchy nose?
How will you explain the lump
Your scaly tail makes on your rump?
And, just to add to all your cares,
I'm cursing all your future heirs.

One from every generation
Doomed to Rat-elimination.
So when at last the last Bignose is
Pushing up the graveyard roses,
Old Nick will rise and be re-born

To claim the splinter from his horn.
Ratspell, Sprattspell, Blackspellation
Doomed to Rat-elimination.

P.S.
By the way, Burt, can you float
A hundred feet above the moat?
Because, Bignose, if you know not how
I'll see you soon – ta ta for now."

With that, she bounced high into the air and, with a blue flash and a purple bang, she and the cat disappeared into the murky depths of the cold, dark moat.

The crowd hung around for a while, clapping and shouting for more. Eventually, as the sun sank behind the castle, they wandered happily homewards.

"What a day!" said Widow Woodbine. "I haven't had such a good time since me husband's funeral. I do enjoy a good curse. I wouldn't be in Sir Burt what-ever-his-name-is' boots for all the ale in Aylesbury."

Darkness crept across the deserted green and with it came the Rats. For them the fair had just begun and what a feast there was spread before them! Roast boars' skulls to rummage in, beef bones to gnaw upon, delicious lumps of fat and gristle. As a young Rat listening to Uncle Sharkie tell the story, my mouth would water at the pickings from Burt's medieval fair.

"And is it really true about the little frog, Uncle Sharkie?" I'd ask.

"As true as a Twopenny Turnip," he'd reply with a wink. "Hopping about amongst the bones was a little green frog who claimed that he was really the Chief Inspector of Villages."

In a little room at the top of the castle, stuffed full of accounts and plans, Pierre le Drain sat up late into the night. He'd helped put the groaning Sir Burt to bed and now he was penning the last few lines of his report on the building of Knotty Oak castle. His trunk was packed and tomorrow, very thankfully, he could return to the court of King Norman. He chewed on his quill and thought about the events of the day. What a strange people these English are, he thought, with their witches and curses and strange food in baskets. And then, for no particular reason, he took a small piece of parchment, headed it "The Bignose Curse", and wrote out Nell's Spell to the very last line.

Lord of the Rats

After a week in bed, Burt got up still feeling ratty. In the mirror he noticed that his hair was beginning to go grey – and had his nose grown even longer? He twitched it a couple of times and smoothed his whiskers. Oddly enough the change in his appearance made him feel better. Scurrying down to the kitchen he ate a whole chicken, bones and all. They taste better with their feathers on, he thought.

The gradual change in the manner and appearance of their Lord was all the talk of

Widow Woodbine's ale house.

"He hardly leaves the castle at all these days," said Firmity Hogswallow. "His poor wife is at her wits' end, what with him skulking about half the night and chewing holes in doors."

"He's off his stump!" declared Harry Clank the blacksmith. "A soldier came into my forge this morning with a notice saying we han't to kill no more Rats, by order of His Lordship. It ain't natural. Rats is there to be killed."

"Mark my words," said Ned the Bread, "summat's got to be done."

I'm pleased to say that my ancestors were not slow to make the most of the situation, and in no time at all the castle was all but overrun with Rats. Burt's family begged him to change his mind. He only stared at them with his one black beady eye and hissed through yellowing teeth:

"The Rats be my friends and not a hair on their heads shall be hurted."

*   *   *

When Lady Bignose found a nest in her best winter wimple, she decided she'd had enough and left the castle. The rest of the family went with her and were quickly followed by the soldiers with Rat holes in their boots. Burt was left alone with his friends.

So what happened inside the castle that led to Burt's final downfall? Your history says he simply went mad and jumped. That's not the story that Uncle Sharkie told to me. He said that the curse turned and twisted Burt into a thing that was neither man nor Rat, with matted fur, long scratchy claws and clothes that hung in rags.

"At night," said Uncle Sharkie, "he would scuttle about his empty passageways, hissing and twitching his great nose, dragging his scaly tail behind him like a snake."

For a while Burt was accepted by the Rats as a sort of honorary member of the tribe. "After all," Uncle Sharkie explained, "his tail and whiskers were a great improvement from a Rat's point of view and he was quite happy to share his store of corn."

But trouble began to brew when the Rats decided they didn't like Burt's cooking. Every day Burt boiled up his share of corn, with a few old boots for flavour, in a huge iron pot in the kitchen. After a while, it seemed he needed a little more than boots in his soup. Rats began to disappear. When things were looked into it is said that bones were found amongst the laces and nails at the bottom of Burt's pot. Had he been prowling the castle looking for friends to

drop in for supper? Who knows. The Rats
declared him to be "vermin" and word was
passed through the walls that he was to be
hunted down. Burt soon sensed the change. As
he skulked through his halls and galleries he
could feel a growing tide of Rats in the walls
around him. He was hunted for a day and most
of a night through every crack and cranny in

the castle – upwards, floor by floor, until there was nowhere left to hide and the Lord of Knotty Oak was trapped on the roof of his castle's highest turret.

When the first light caught the top of the castle battlements, Burt was standing with his back against the flagpole. Frost sparkled on his tattered rags. For an hour he had stared, unmoving, at the bolted trap door. Now it quivered with a rasping, scraping sound. Holes were growing along its edges, under the hinges, around the rat-rattling bolt. Whiskers! . . . Small pink noses! . . . Sharp yellow teeth! The trap door collapsed into a heaving grey mass. A scrabbling wave of Rats welled up from below and rushed towards the figure crouched by the flagpole.

The screeching frightened the villagers from their beds. They rubbed their eyes and peered up from doors and windows. High above the castle, something was climbing towards the tattered Bignose flag that hung from the swaying flagpole. Whatever it was reached the flag and clung to it, screaming down at something they couldn't see.

"No! No! I be your friend. No! No! No!!"

. . . Crack! A ratlike shriek. The pole toppled over the battlements and plunged like an arrow thirty metres into the moat. Later, the villagers fished out the flagpole – chewed clean through at the base, but of Sir Burt Bignose, Lord of Knotty Oak, not a whisker was ever found.

One from Every Generation

Eventually, Lady Bignose and her family moved back into Knotty Oak Castle. She ordered the soldiers to chase out the Rats. They did their best, but my ancestors were tunnelled so deep in the walls they would have had to pull down the castle stone by stone to be rid of them all.

Burt's eldest son, Ethelburt, was still a boy, so for a while Lady Bignose looked after the Manor and life was easier for the villagers.

But as Ethelburt grew to manhood it became clear that he had inherited not only his father's nose, but his grasping, greedy nature. Luckily for the villagers, they didn't have to put up with him for long. Young Sir Ethelburt spent much of his time on what your history calls "Crusades", which meant a lot of charging about stealing things in foreign parts. On his last crusade, Sir Ethelburt's horse put a hoof in a Rathole in the Holy Land and the second Lord of Knotty Oak never recovered from the trip.

And so, generation by generation, the curse tailed the family down through the ages. For instance, Ethelburt's great-grandson died of a poisoned bite from a Rat nesting in his helmet. It served him right, in my opinion, for sticking his big nose where it wasn't wanted.

His great-great-grandson breathed his last on

his way home from a pilgrimage to see the Pope in Rome. He had stopped for the night at a French inn and, while he slept, a short-sighted Rat by the name of Camembert began rummaging about in the bedclothes for crumbs. A huge snort from a Bignose nose put Camembert in such a panic that he mistook the open Bignose mouth for a place of safety, a fatal mistake for all concerned. The curse had struck again. I always felt very sorry for Camembert, but Uncle Sharkie would laugh like a drain whenever he told the story.

"It served him right," he said. "A French Rat should have known better than to look for something worth eating in the bed of an Englishman."

The curse wasn't always so obvious, for many Bignoses were victims of the Black Death, a plague that your scientists say is carried by the Rat flea. They don't bother to mention that the Plague was just as deadly to my ancestors and that people of those times probably had more fleas than the Rats.

Towards the end of the reign of Queen Elizabeth the First, a Tudor Bignose was killed by a piece of the family coat of arms, a horrible carving of a Rat crushed beneath a spurred boot. It fell on his head as he was tapping out his pipe on the mantelpiece. He had taken up the new craze of smoking tobacco. He died whispering the family motto *"Spe certa quid splattus Rattus rattus"* (there is nothing better than a squashed Rat). So you could say that he was one of the first of your tribe to die from your ridiculous habit of smoking. Since then, I'm pleased to say, tobacco has probably done for far more Bignoses than Nell's curse.

In the eighteenth century, the curse claimed two generations at once when old Eli Bignose, out threshing the harvest, had a couple of Rats run up the legs of his breeches. The sight of the

old man leaping around the yard, breeches
bulging with Rats, caused his nephew to laugh
so much that he fell off the rick and broke his
neck. The violent exercise proved too much for
old Eli's heart. The Rats, you'll be pleased to
know, survived, one of them to a great age. In
later years he would often recount his ordeal in
old Eli Bignose's smelly old breeches.

By the time Isambard Bignose was born, the
family had fallen on hard times. They had lost
their title in the sixteenth century for backing
the wrong king and lost their fortune early in

the nineteenth century when Isambard's father, Jasper Bignose, backed the wrong horse. Knotty Oak Castle, battered by wars and time and rebuilt by generations of Bignoses, was almost a ruin, and the old village with its green had crumbled away and become a walled garden.

Now, if I were to tell you that Isambard was a bit odd, you'd say, "Of course you'd think that – you're a Rat." Well, I don't claim to be an expert on human behaviour, but it doesn't seem normal to me that young Isambard spent every waking hour murdering Rats in the old castle dungeons. He was obsessed with his search for a deadly Rat poison. For years his experiments came to nothing. Then, during a short holiday shooting deer in the Scottish Highlands, Isambard became violently ill. Had he died, the lives of millions of my tribe might have been spared. Sadly, he survived to turn misfortune into gold by tracing the cause of his illness to a breakfast of stale porridge, served by a canny crofter. Less than a year later, Isambard was

manufacturing poison by the tonne from a fungus he'd discovered growing on rotting porridge, and RAT-ROT (the name still makes my tail stand on end) was beginning to strike fear into the hearts of Rats all over the world.

By the age of thirty, Isambard had built RAT-

ROT factories in every corner of the British Empire, with huge estates in Scotland growing porridge oats.

With his fortune, Isambard pulled down most of the old castle and built Rat-Rot Hall, to his own design – a wonderful monster of a place. Downwind, because of the awful smell of rotting porridge, he built his latest factory in the same style. He felled the great oaks that grew in the park around the Hall, and in their place rose Knotty Oak Villas, cheap back-to-back houses for his workers. The moat became part of a canal that carried Rat-Rot to all parts of the country and the world beyond.

The Rats found the new house and factory very comfortable and they soon moved into the back-to-backs of Knotty Oak Villas.

"Bloomin' marvellous," grumbled Isambard's workers. "Whoever heard of a Rat poison manufacturer whose houses were overrun with Rats? The more Rat-Rot we put down for them, the better the little beggars seem to like it."

After years of Isambard's experiments, the Rats of Knotty Oak were immune to his most deadly poison.

This was our golden age. Stowed away amongst RAT-ROT cargoes, the Knotty Oak Rats rode the barges, sailed the ships and colonized the world – India, China, the Americas. By the same route some returned, rich with stories and romance of faraway places, from the steamy sewers of Singapore to the rubbish heaps of Rio, by the dustbins of Dundee. Such tales, passed down to our storytellers and told on nights around the stone, filled me with a longing to travel and see for myself the world that lay beyond the garden walls.

The Devil in the Fountain

Queen Victoria was worried about the Rats in Windsor Castle. The Rats weren't worried about Queen Victoria; they'd been in residence at least as long as the Royal Family and considered it as much their home as hers. It made no difference. At the Royal Command, RAT-ROT wiped them out to the very last Rat. The Queen was so pleased with this mass murder that the Bignose title was restored.

To celebrate the family's good fortune, Sir Isambard Bignose commissioned a magnificent bronze fountain as a centrepiece for his garden:

King Neptune rising majestically from the waves, surrounded by gambolling mermaids (modelled on the Queen and a large cod) mounted on prancing sea horses (modelled on the Prime Minister, Mr Gladstone).

When the workmen cleared the centre of the garden for the fountain, they came across a small rounded stone that they couldn't move.

"At first I thought it was a bloomin' great toadstool," said the foreman.

The head gardener looked at it nervously. "That's the Devil's Stone. It's best left alone. You won't shift it anyway."

The foreman prodded the stone with his boot. "What, that little thing? Our new steam hammer'll crack it like a nut."

Two days and three new steam hammers later, the workmen admitted defeat. King Neptune and company were hoisted into place right on top of the stone. The walls and terraces around the pond were built from the ruins of the old castle. So, once again the "Tip of the

Devil's Horn" was encircled by its ancient stones.

To show off his wonderful new home, Sir Isambard arranged a grand fancy dress ball with fireworks, electric light and hundreds of important people.

The great occasion arrived, boilers were stoked, steam-pumps hissed impatiently. When the orchestra struck up "God Save the Queen", Lady Bignose released a bottle of champagne, which smashed against Neptune's mighty chest and the fountain burst into life. What a spectacle! How it spouted and sparkled. Higher and higher, until the costumes of the cheering guests were soaked with spray. Nervously, they pushed backwards as the fountain began to get out of hand. Many important people were trodden into the mud in a confusion of spray and rockets, exploding light bulbs and steam. Desperately, Sir Isambard pulled levers and closed valves but the fountain didn't stop until the roof blew off the boiler house. The evening was not a success.

Later, Lady Bignose swore that the fountain had come to life.

"What nonsense," said Sir Isambard, but although he had the boiler repaired, he never risked another display.

For the rest of his life, Sir Isambard travelled the world, shooting and collecting things. He came home every Christmas with crates of stuffed animals and strange objects. As the years went by the house became so full that his wife and children were forced to live in the attics.

On Sir Isambard's final Christmas, everything was as usual. The goose had been eaten and the Christmas pudding was served. "Mind you eat it all, dear," said his wife with an odd giggle. "I've put something special in it for you." Thinking that she had followed the old tradition of stirring in a silver threepenny bit, Sir Isambard ate it to the last crumb.

"I don't appear to have been lucky this year," were his last words. Driven mad by the neverending dusting of dead animals, Lady Bignose had put RAT-ROT in his pudding.

The news that Sir Isambard had died by his own poison was greeted with great rejoicing by Rats all over the world. Even today, we Rats still celebrate Christmas as "Lady Bignose Day". The dear lady was quietly locked away in a home for dotty gentlefolk and the children were sent to live with relatives.

Sir Neville Bignose, Isambard's eldest son, went to an uncle in India and eventually became something high up in the Diplomatic Service. One evening, towards the end of his career, he was dining at the hunting lodge of the Rajah of Bungalowbill in the foothills of the Pyjamacush. The meal had just begun and they were discussing the day's tiger shoot when a Rat, whose name, I am ashamed to say, I cannot pronounce, fell from the thatched roof into Sir Neville's mulligatawny. In shocked silence, the two old enemies stared at each other, Sir Neville dripping and the Rat treading hot soup.

Now, in my opinion, the correct thing to do in such circumstances would be to have politely asked the Rat to leave the table. Not Sir Neville. Grabbing a carving knife, he brought it down with all his strength on the uninvited guest swimming in his first course.

"Oh, jolly good show, old chap," shouted the Rajah and led his guests in polite applause. Sir Neville smiled a sickly smile at the Rajah and then at the murdered Rat, impaled on the bamboo table. Steam rose, pieces of soup plate winked in the soft light of the Tilly lamp.

"I believe I've stabbed myself in the knee," he said. The wound wasn't serious but to Sir Neville, I am glad to say, it proved as lethal as a bite from a King Cobra.

Colonel Bogey

Now, I will admit that all storytellers add a little colour to the telling of a tale and this tale has travelled down many a year and been retold many a time, so how much should you believe? Well, before you make up your mind, perhaps you'd better hear the tale of Albert, the last of the Bignoses, most of which I know the truth of, for I play no small part in it myself.

By the time Albert was born, the Bignoses no longer believed in the curse. Even Sir Neville, as he lay dying from his poisoned knee, dismissed it as "a lot of superstitious mumbo-jumbo".

Albert was the youngest of Sir Neville's three sons. He grew up in India but, unlike his father, he hated the heat and was allergic to curry. Albert was a tall, dopy-looking boy with a particularly fine example of the family nose. It hung on his head like a large beak and made him lean forward when he walked. Fortunately, his huge feet kept him from falling on his face. He spent his boyhood sitting in the shade, dreaming of cold, wet places and cucumbers. Because of his magnificent feet and a natural talent for losing things, Albert became an officer in the Army Stores and Signals.

If you'd asked his fellow officers what they thought of Albert, they'd have said, "Awfully nice chap. OK at his job, I suppose, but as dull and dusty as the inside of a broom cupboard."

This would have pleased Albert. It was just what he wanted them to think, because Albert had a secret – he had a wicked sense of humour. Beneath his dusty camouflage, he spent his time in the Army making a joke out of the mountains of paperwork that landed on his desk. He burrowed around in it, like a malevolent mole, forging an order here, diverting a memo there. When soldiers in the desert received Teddy Bear hot water bottles, or commandos on Arctic manoeuvres were issued with day-glo leopard-skin bikinis, the one man the Army would never suspect sat behind his desk quietly laughing his oversized socks off.

Albert's biggest fear was that the Army might one day call upon him to shoot someone.

Speaking as a Rat that has been shot at a time or two, I've always thought that this was to Albert's credit. With a little paper shuffling and a well-aimed rubber stamp or two, Albert ordered himself to be posted to cold, wet places where the action wasn't. In the same way, he gradually promoted himself to Colonel. Because the cold and wet always decorated Albert's nose with an icicle or dewdrop, he became known throughout his regiment as Colonel Bogey.

Colonel Bogey, alias Albert, only slipped up once. He forgot to seal an order in which he issued a very important general with a Dennis the Menace water pistol. The dispatch rider who opened and read the order was a Scot, a small angry carrot of a man called Dougal McPile. Private McPile never missed a trick. He wrote a note to Colonel Bogey, threatening to tell all to the General unless the Colonel made him his batman (which, in case you don't know, is what the army call a sort of personal servant). Although the Colonel pretended to be shocked, he thought it was a great joke.

"What's this note all about, Private McPile?"

"Blackmail, Sirr."

"You realize that blackmail is a serious matter, McPile?"

"Yes, Sirr."

"You wouldn't like to change your mind, I suppose?"

"Noo, Sirr."

"Very well, McPile. Since you've forced me

into making you my batman, then Batman you shall be." And from that moment he never called him anything else.

How different would have been my tale if Colonel Bogey had remembered to seal his order. We Rats would never have had to suffer the curse of Batman the Bad.

The Colonel's one regret was that he never married. He met ladies in his younger days, usually at dances in the officers' club, but he could never think of the right thing to say. Once he'd upset a major's daughter by telling her that she reminded him of Attila, a pet hen he'd had as a boy. Real friendship blossomed only once. Primrose was a tall girl with a nose almost as big as his own. They met for a few weeks and she seemed to enjoy his company. Albert often thought how his life might have been if he hadn't asked her to dance. At first he'd held her at arm's length, placing his feet as carefully as a tap dancer in a minefield. She smiled at him encouragingly. Recklessly he held her closer. Their noses clashed like a couple of sparring toucans, her glasses fell beneath his boots and were scrunched as flat as a steam-rollered bicycle. By the time he dared show his face at another dance, Primrose had found a partner with smaller feet.

I've been uncomfortably close to the Colonel's gigantic boots more than once myself and I can only wonder at Primrose's courage in agreeing to dance with him in the first place.

Rat-Rot Hall

About the time Albert promoted himself to Colonel, his eldest brother, Sir Clive Bignose, died suddenly in India of Mongolian Mumps. His second brother, Freddy, had always been a bit wild and the unexpected inheritance went to his head. Over the next few years he guzzled, gambled and gave away just about all the RAT-ROT empire. Only the house and factory at Knotty Oak were left and they would have gone the same way if it hadn't been for Freddy's obsession with cricket.

The Colonel was stationed in the Outer

Hebrides when he read the news in the *Times*. He was in his quarters with his feet up in front of the fire. The only sounds were the rain beating against the windows and the low grumble of Batman McPile ironing handkerchiefs.

"Good grief!" said the Colonel, sitting up. "Brother Freddy's been bowled out. Listen to this, Batman – 'International playboy, Sir Freddy Bignose, heir to the RAT-ROT empire, was killed yesterday while trying to land his seaplane on the pitch during the test at Lords. Australia appealed against the state of the wicket and the match was declared a draw.' Well bless my soul . . . poor old Freddy."

"Och! That's dreadful news, Colonel," said Batman McPile.

"Yes, it certainly is," replied the Colonel. "It means that England will probably lose the Ashes."

I've often wondered what these precious ashes were. When I asked Uncle Sharkie he said,

"Forget it, Spratt – nothing about cricket could ever make sense to a Rat."

For a long time, Albert stared out at the rain. Neither brother Clive, nor poor old brother Freddy had any children. He was now Colonel Sir Albert Bignose, heir to what was left of the RAT-ROT empire – and the last of the Bignoses. Thoughtfully he turned to Batman McPile.

"Batman, if I was to arrange for the Army to retire us both, how would you like to be chief steward to the Manor of Knotty Oak?"

Batman put down his iron. "I'd like it fine for five pounds a week and a new pair of boots at Christmas." Carefully he folded a handkerchief the size of a small tablecloth and placed it on top of the heap . . . "And you can iron your own ruddy hankies – Sirr."

Knotty Oak was no longer a village. It had been swallowed up by the city that had once been some distance away. The Colonel recognized

nothing on the drive from the station until the taxi dropped them in front of the house. As a small boy on holiday from India, he'd been allowed to peer through the great wrought iron gates at the ancestral home. He'd never forgotten it. The same rat gargoyles glared down through twisted chimneys. Slate roofs rose like mossy cliffs amongst turrets and spires stuffed with twigs and peppered with jackdaws. As far as he knew, the house had been shut up since the poisoning of Grandfather Isambard.

Colonel Bogey couldn't wait to get inside.

"Look at it, Batman – isn't it wonderful? And we've got the whole place to ourselves." Which of course was true if you didn't count my tribe, the Rats.

Batman McPile had to saw through the padlock on the gates and it took the two of them to force open the double doors of the great hall. But what a sight when they stepped inside! The light came from a huge stained-glass window that told the colourful story of

RAT-ROT, from the sowing of the oats for porridge to the death agonies of the poor Rats. The walls were hung with herds of animal heads, forests of antlers, crocodiles, swordfish, shrunken heads and enough weapons for a small army. A stuffed elephant stood by the stairs, stuffed birds stared out from glass cases, roosted in the rafters or soared among the chandeliers. Over everything lay a blanket of years of dust and dead spiders. The Colonel felt that he'd come home at last.

"It's perfect," he sighed, "just perfect."

But Batman McPile didn't think it was perfect. As he got used to the gloom, he noticed small grey shapes that glided between shadows. Faint squeaks and scuttlings came from every corner of the hall.

"Well, I wouldn't stay here for all the porridge in Perthshire."

"What the Devil is it?" whispered the Colonel.

Batman McPile shuddered. "Rats, Sir! The whole place is alive with Rats."

It took a small army to repair the damage of time and weather on the old house – in fact a platoon of soldiers from the Colonel's old regiment. Before he left, he'd forged an order transferring them to Knotty Oak for "indefinite manoeuvres". The work took many months but no one minded. The cellars were full of wine and a good time was had by all. After a final party in the great hall, they left with the Colonel's thanks and as many bottles as they could carry.

The Rats didn't leave as easily. This was the time known in our history as "The First Battle of Batman the Bad". When he found that RAT-ROT had no effect, Batman tried Isambard's huge collection of Rat-traps in the cellars. The cellar Rats had studied these traps for years. They would set them off and squeal until Batman came running to find another empty trap. This battle of wits went on for months and Batman was just about beaten, when he found his most deadly weapon in the small ads of the *Shooting Times*. It read:

FOR SALE – JACK RUSSELL PUPPIES
PARTICULARLY RECOMMENDED FOR
RATTING

It was my great-grandfather who told me that, even as a puppy, Bertrund the Beast was a killer. He said that from the day Bertrund arrived, nowhere in the house or garden was safe. The Rats retreated to the fountain, where even Bertrund couldn't get them, and for a while there was an uneasy truce.

Sir Isambard's wonderful fountain was our fortress. It had been a refuge for generations of Rats. Later, it was home for me and my family and that's how we thought it would always be. The fountain was first occupied more than half a century before, when winter frosts cracked one of the pipes that ran from the pump-house. When the first brave souls ventured inside, they found a vast bronze cavern. Pipes coiled up and around like a spaghetti maze that could take them to every corner of the fountain. They found caves and crannies that were the insides of breaking waves or the hollow curves of a mermaid's tail – and they found the Devil's Stone. Our Storytellers said it would be there and there it was. The Stone glowed with a faint yellow light – too dim for the human eye, but bright enough for a Rat to see that it still bore the mark of the axe of Sir Burt Bignose, the first Lord of Knotty Oak.

The Battle of Bowler Hat

Batman and Colonel Bogey settled into their own ways. Batman never did move into Rat-Rot Hall, instead he made himself very comfortable in the pump-house. He grew vegetables and fought battles with the garden shrubbery. What a sight he was in his kilt, string vest and army boots, brandishing a claymore captured by the Colonel's ancestors at the battle of Dunroamin! Colonel Bogey spent his time hidden in clouds of dust in the library, digging up his family tree and sneezing his way through rolls of ancient parchment, or clambering through rooms crammed from floor to ceiling, listing the treasures he found. In summer he grew cucumbers and sat on the terrace by the fountain, feeding cheese and onion crisps to the sparrows and laughing at Batman as he battered the shrubbery with his claymore.

Little changed for the Rats in the fountain. They never went near the house and the garden was always a dangerous place in daylight. My great-grandfather said that Bertrund the Beast grew more cunning with every year that passed, and you had to keep a sharp eye out, or Batman

might take a pop at you from the shrubbery. At first he used an elephant gun and blasted holes in the fountain. The Colonel soon put a stop to it ("Too loud, too dangerous and you're frightening the sparrows"), so Batman took to using an Apache bow and arrow he found in the umbrella stand.

Time passed. The RAT-ROT factory closed down. The back-to-backs of old Knotty Oak were bulldozed away and tower blocks began to peer over the walls like nosy neighbours. None of this bothered the old soldiers. The garden was like an island; its massive old walls kept out the noise and chaos of the world that flowed around them.

Nothing disturbed their peace until a letter dropped into the box by the gate. It lay like an unexploded bomb, waiting for Batman when he checked the box a few weeks later.

The letter was from Reginald T. Smugden,

Chief Clerk. It stated that the house, factory and garden were to be compulsorily purchased by a consortium of the Borough Council and Grabbold & Nickett Inc., to be developed into a Colossal Consumer Hyper-Household Mega Mall. Batman stared at the letter.

"Is that English?"

"Some of it," sighed the Colonel.

"Well, what does it mean?"

"It means the blighters want to buy us up, chuck us out and build a ruddy great shop!"

"Whoooooott?" screamed Batman. He grabbed the letter and tore it to pieces. "Never!!" He screwed it into a ball and jumped up and down on it. "Over my . . . dead . . . body . . ."

Bertrund the Beast joined in the attack on the paper ball.

"Snap! Snarl! Snap!"

"Ouch!" roared Batman. "He's bitten through ma' best tartan slippers."

Batman hopped around holding his leg.

Bertrund dived under the settee with the screwed-up letter and chewed it to a pulp.

"Calm yourself, man," ordered the Colonel. "Sit down, I'll make a pot of tea and we'll decide what is to be done."

While the Colonel bandaged his wounds, Batman waved his claymore and planned their campaign.

"Mines in the front drive (ouch!). Man traps in the shrubbery (ahh!). Cannons! . . . Catapults! . . . (ouch!). Boiling oil . . . Blunderbusses . . ." The Colonel tied a knot in the bandage and worried about his cucumbers.

More letters arrived from Reginald T. Smugden, each more threatening than the last. Men in suits, carrying briefcases, lurked around the gates in ever-increasing numbers until at last the great man himself appeared. He was large and pasty-faced, long-black-coated and shiny-shoed, his bespectacled eyes like dead fish in a bowl. The Chief Clerk stood still before the padlocked gate. Briefcases snapped and fussed around him. Then, as if money had been put in a slot, an arm came up, holding a loud-hailer.

"Reginald T. Smugden here . . . Chief Clerk . . . Very busy man . . . Won't beat around the bush . . . Have given repeated warnings . . . Must suffer the consequences . . . Eviction by force . . . Nine o'clock Monday morning . . . repeat, nine o'clock Monday morning . . . you have . . ."

"Swoosh!" an Apache arrow took off his bowler hat.

"Thunk!" Another punctured his briefcase. Pin-striped suits surrounded him and he was carried off to his shiny black car.

"Round one to us," chuckled Batman. "We'd better be ready for round two on Monday morning."

"We Rats didn't know what was going on," said my great-grandfather. "But it was a great joke to see someone else shot at for a change."

Batman staggered to the hall table and dumped more weapons on the huge pile he'd already collected. Colonel Bogey looked at his watch. "Surely that's enough, Batman – it's nearly midnight. Sit down and drink your cocoa."

Batman slumped into a chair.

"Och, I need something stronger than cocoa."

"You should have thought of that before you nailed up the cellar door."

He'd spent the day barricading doors and windows and hauling a small brass cannon on to the roof.

"Not that it'll make any difference in the end," sighed the Colonel.

Batman bristled. "We're not beaten yet, ye know."

"Just a matter of time." The Colonel felt old and tired. He pointed at the pile of weapons on the table . . . "And anyway, I'm no good at this sort of thing. Always fought my battles with pen and paper, not guns and swords."

They stared at the fire in gloomy silence. Around them the old house seemed settled and peaceful. Logs fell softly in the grate. Bertrund snored like a small pig on the hearth. Afterwards, the Colonel could never remember how it happened. Did he fall asleep? Was it in a dream that the idea came to him? He knew that some time later he sat up suddenly with a complete plan in his head.

"Batman! Wake up!"

"Wha . . . Wha . . . What day is it?"

"Nearly Saturday. We've got to move fast—"

"But . . . but . . . but . . ."

"Or we won't get to the Town Hall before it gets light."

"Town Hall? . . . But . . . err . . . it's on the other side of the city . . . Bailiffs watching the gate . . . we haven't—"

"Yes, yes. I've thought of all that," said Colonel Bogey, jumping up impatiently. "Look, if we could get to the Town Hall without being seen, could you get us in?"

"Aye . . . nae problem," said Batman.

The legend of the headless camel was one of my favourite stories as a young Rat. This strange creature, with two humps and short front legs, appeared one night in the garden. It staggered about for a while before struggling over the wall, making loud grunting noises and disappearing into the canal. But the story always puzzled me until I realized that it must have been Batman and Colonel Bogey with rucksacks on their backs, launching the dug-out canoe. The canoe had last been used by a Borneo head-hunter. It wasn't designed to be shoved over a wall but somehow they managed it and paddled six kilometres to where the canal ran past the back of the Town Hall.

Soot black, bat-haunted and pigeon-roosted, the back wall of the Town Hall was not a pretty sight. It rose like a grimy cliff, straight up from the canal. Batman unpacked the grappling hook.

"There are bars on the windows till the third floor. It'll no be an easy climb."

What was "no an easy climb" for Batman very nearly killed the Colonel, but he made it, and I for one reckon he deserved a medal. The very thought of it makes me giddy. Covered in muck and feathers, he hauled himself up to the window and collapsed over the sill. By the time he'd got his breath back, Batman had found the office.

"You've never seen anything like it. The size of a football pitch with REGINALD T. SMUGDEN, CHIEF CLERK in big gold letters on the door. A great mahogany desk and enough files to stretch from here to Inverness."

The sight of all the neatly labelled filing cabinets gladdened Colonel Bogey's heart. Here was something he understood. He opened the nearest, marked "A", and beamed in at its contents. Batman set to work on the safe he'd found behind a painting of the great man himself.

They worked through the night, all the next day and, after a few hours' sleep on the floor, on through the whole of Sunday. By three o'clock on Monday morning, they had done all they could. Very tired, but in no way down-hearted, they lowered themselves from the window and paddled the leaking canoe back along the canal. The sun rose and the canoe sank as the two climbed over the old garden wall. Back at the Town Hall, in the safe behind the painting, was a large envelope marked FOR THE URGENT ATTENTION OF REGINALD T. SMUGDEN, CHIEF CLERK.

Too excited to sleep, Batman and the Colonel sat by the fire in the hall and waited to see what the morning would bring. The hours dragged by, nine o'clock came and went, ten o'clock, eleven and still no shining black cars drew up outside the gates of Rat-Rot Hall. By twelve o'clock they were sure they had won the Battle of the Bowler Hat.

I would love to have seen Reginald's face when he opened his safe on Monday morning. He slumped behind his huge mahogany desk. In front of him was the envelope. It had contained three letters and a note with a fiver pinned to it. He held one of the letters in his shaking hand. He couldn't believe it. It was apparently from

himself to Sir Albert Bignose, saying that the Council no longer wanted the Colonel's house and garden, but were offering to buy his old factory, which they wished to preserve as the Waterloo Home for Old Soldiers. It went on to say that this had been made possible by the donation of a large cheque from a Swiss Bank by an anonymous benefactor. The letter ended with a perfect forgery of the Chief Clerk's signature.

The second letter was addressed to Reginald's bank in Switzerland, instructing them to donate £250,000 from his secret account to the Borough Council's Fund for Old Soldiers.

The third letter informed the Council that he, Reginald T. Smugden, Chief Clerk, was handing in his notice as, due to unforeseen circumstances he was leaving for South America as soon as possible.

Reginald took an immaculate handkerchief from his top pocket and mopped his fat, pasty face. He wiped his glasses, picked up the note and read it again. The letters might have been a horrible joke but for this dreadful piece of paper. It informed him that enough evidence had been found in his files to prove that he had been on the fiddle for years. Copies had been made of all incriminating documents so if he didn't want to be Reginald T. Smugden, Chief Convict, he had better post all three letters right away. There was a P.S. at the bottom with an arrow pointing to the fiver. It said, "Please accept this as a contribution towards a new bowler hat." This was Batman's idea, although I'm fairly sure it wasn't his fiver.

For the last time in his life, Reginald T. Smugden pressed the button on his intercom. When his secretary answered, he said, "I'm just popping out for a while, Miss Philadelphia. Please make absolutely sure that you post the three letters in my out tray and would you book a one-way flight to Rio de Janeiro for tomorrow morning."

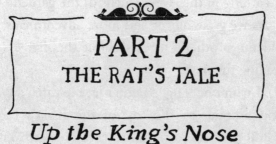

PART 2
THE RAT'S TALE

Up the King's Nose

I was born in a nest in the end of King Neptune's nose. Not the usual place for a nursery, I'll admit, but from a Rat's point of view it was warm and comfortable and just about the safest place in the fountain. Growing up in a nose did have its problems. It could get very hot on sunny days and my mother was always worrying that one of us would fall out through the nostrils. But I remember many peaceful summer evenings when we would lie in our nest and listen to the blackbird singing from the top of Neptune's trident and every now and then the nest would suddenly fill with cool wafts of air, as if the old king were breathing in the sweet smells of the garden.

As we grew bigger and more adventurous, so did my mother's threats about the dangers of leaving the nest.

"I won't be long, so don't let me catch any of you nipping to the top of the King's head. You'll get pecked by those cheeky sparrows or carried off by a magpie like poor cousin Rita." My mother had an endless supply of accident-prone relatives.

"Remember your daft uncle Roland, stuck in the pipes for a week before he was slim enough to slide down."

"Yes, Mum," we'd say, and as soon as she'd gone, we were up the pipes quicker than you could say "Hickory Dickory Dock."

I got my first glimpse of the garden through the spikes of the old king's crown. To me, it looked like a small forest. Twisted oaks and tangled shrubbery clambered over by Old

Man's-Beard and brambles. The lawn at the front of the house was a meadow, speckled with flowers and butterflies. The water garden, where the spring drained into the canal, was a bog splashed with yellow iris and zigzagged by dragonflies.

We had sneaked up to the top of the king's head on the day we got our first sight of the enemy. We couldn't believe it. Batman in his kilt and string vest, Colonel Bogey with his huge nose and bald head – surely these weren't the creatures of our worst nightmares. They didn't look dangerous at all, they looked funny. We began to giggle. We giggled so much that Bertrund heard us and his barking sent us scuttling back down to safety. However you looked at him, Bertrund the Beast was no joke.

The fountain was a great place for a young Rat. It was a maze of pipes, all shapes and sizes, with a thousand places to hide. Where else could you dive head first down a pipe and slide from Queen Victoria's head to Mr Gladstone

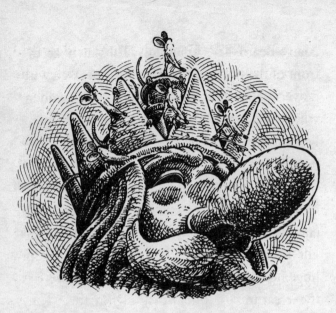

the seahorse's nose? It was like an adventure
playground inside a bronze cathedral.

But I liked it best on winter evenings around
the Stone. When the wind blew and the rain
rattled on the old fountain, it would hum, very
softly, like a giant bell. The whole tribe would
gather in a circle, the youngest next to the
Stone, for it was always warm, even on the
coldest night. Our storytellers sat in the groove
on the top, telling us the tale of Burt Bignose,

or stories of travel and adventure in ships and foreign lands. When I grew up I wanted, more than anything, to be a traveller and a teller of tales. Unfortunately, I never grew up.

It was my own fault. I'd been told over and over never to go into the garden in daylight. From the top of the king's head it all looked so peaceful and the hazelnuts were ripe. Every breeze would send a shower of fat, brown nuts bouncing on to the terrace. I could just nip out, grab a nut and be back in two shakes of a Rat's tail.

When I reached the trees I had a good look around. Nothing. The whole world seemed to be dozing in the sunshine. There isn't anything like the taste of a fresh hazelnut. Just a quick nibble, I thought. A slight breeze. A large nut bounced on the stones next to me. I looked up. SNAP! Bertrund's teeth closed like a gin-trap a fraction above my neck. If he'd been younger I wouldn't have lived to tell the tale.

Run! He was snapping at my heels all across

the terrace . . . twist! . . . turn! . . . nowhere to hide . . . panic! . . . a tin . . . by the bench. I was inside before I had time to think.

Batman was very fond of tinned mackerel. He'd opened the tin with his army knife the day before and eaten his lunch with a fork. It wasn't like him to leave tins about, so I suppose I was lucky. It didn't feel lucky to be bounced around the terrace by Bertrund the Beast. He couldn't get at me past the spiky top so, after a lot of snarling and swearing, he pushed the tin into the hot sun and sat down to wait.

Inside the tin it soon felt like an oven. It got hotter as the afternoon wore on until I was sure I would be cooked alive. Bertrund didn't move. Slowly the shadows crept across the stones towards me. It seemed an age before the sun slipped behind the hazel bushes and the tin began to cool.

I'm sure Bertrund would have stayed on guard all night if Batman hadn't called.

"Betrund!" He twitched one ear but didn't move. "Where are ye, ye little beastie?" I heard Batman's army boots crunch on the steps. "So there you are. Always disappear on bath night, don't ye?" It was Bertrund's bath night! . . . I was saved! There was a furious snarling as he was picked up by the scruff of the neck. Batman laughed.

"Och come on, it's noo as bad as all that."

Boots scraped again, as if he had turned to go. I held my breath. Then . . .

"Hello, what's this?" The tin was lifted up. "I must have forgotten it. Och well, it's soon got rid of." The tin was flying. Over and over. Through the whistling air. Crash! The top of a tree. Bonk! Bonk! Bonk! from side to side, down through the branches. Thunk! The tin landed upright in the mud where the spring drained into the canal. When my head stopped spinning, I tried to climb out but I was too small to push past the spiky top of the tin. I was trapped.

My family searched the fountain and garden for three days before giving me up for lost. It was Uncle Sharkie who found me. I still don't know how. The first thing he did was dump me into the pond. I sank. I didn't care if I drowned as long as I could drink and drink. When he fished me out by the tail, the smell was still so bad that none of my family would come near me. Uncle Sharkie cared for me until I recovered, but the shock had stopped me growing. Thereafter my brothers and sisters called me

Spratt because of my size and the smell of rotten fish. Gradually the smell wore off but not the name. I was stuck with it.

Uncle Sharkie was the largest Rat I have ever seen. He was dark, almost black, but with a grey muzzle. He had appeared in the garden as a young Rat, saying he was from a branch of the family that had left many years before. His knowledge of our history and wonderful storytelling amazed every Rat that heard him and he was welcomed into the tribe. But there was something odd about him that you couldn't quite put your paw on. Though he saved my life and helped me through difficult times, we never became close friends. When he asked me to become his apprentice, I felt honoured and surprised. I told him there was nothing I wanted more, but was he sure he wanted me?

"Because of your size? What does that matter? A storyteller can be whatever size they choose. You are quick and keen to learn. That is all I ask."

Uncle Sharkie was a hard master. Every word he taught me had to be learned by heart. My mother used to say that I'd forget my tail if it wasn't tied to me and yet, after only one hearing, I could memorize stories that took more than an hour in the telling. From morn 'til night we would sit with our backs to the Stone. I would listen and question, never feeling tired, until Uncle Sharkie would say, "Enough, young Spratt. Off to your nest. You've worn me out with all your chatter."

It seemed to me that my apprenticeship had hardly begun when Uncle Sharkie announced, "Tomorrow night, Spratt, you will take your place on the Stone." I pleaded that I wasn't ready, had a cold, must tidy my nest, but he wouldn't listen.

When my turn came the next evening, my legs shook so much that I needed help to climb the Stone. The young Rats at the front giggled

behind their paws. I looked down at the packed fountain – all my family and friends. Well, Spratt, I thought, this is what you always wanted. Get on with it. At first there were shouts of "Squeak up, we can't hear you at the back," but I kept going and gradually the fountain hushed as the story carried me away. I forgot the crowd, forgot who I was and became a Teller of Tales. At the end there was silence, then a great shout of applause.

"Well done, Spratt!"

"Not bad for a pipsqueak." It felt wonderful. I could tell Uncle Sharkie was pleased.

"Well done, young Spratt. Not bad for your first tale but you've still a lot to learn."

After that, I had a regular place on the Stone. In spite of my size, I became a respected member of the tribe and life in the fountain became easier for me.

Colonel Bogey Smells
a Rat

In the years that followed the raid on the Town Hall, Colonel Bogey and Batman McPile had grown old and as set in their ways as a couple of badgers in a burrow. The Colonel accepted his own offer and sold the old RAT-ROT factory to the Council. He bought a heated greenhouse for all-the-year-round cucumbers and raised Batman's wages to six pounds a week.

"And aboot time too," grumbled Batman. "Ma claymore's all but worn oot – and so am I." He ordered himself the biggest electric hedge-trimmer he could find and happily trimmed away the years.

"He would whizz the odd arrow at us from the shrubbery," my great-grandfather told me, "just to keep his hand in, and sometimes that old beast Bertrund would play round-and-round-the-garden, to keep us on our toes, but mostly we left each other in peace."

Like most storytellers, I'm a bit hazy about dates, but it must have been around the time I told my first tale from the Stone that Batman ended the truce and began his campaign to rid the fountain of Rats. So what was it after so many peaceful years that stirred his old bones to battle? Who was it that persuaded him that my tribe had to be destroyed, once and for all? I'll tell you – it was Pierre le Drain.

When Colonel Bogey wasn't tending his cucumbers, he was burrowing away in the library. He loved the dust and smell, the feel of old books and parchment; ancient chests, trunks, shelves of Rat-nibbled rolls and scrolls, piled from floor to ceiling; hoards of letters, wills, accounts and bills – the scratchings of a thousand quills that inked in the history of the Bignoses. Line by line, chest by trunk, generation by generation, the Colonel had rummaged his way back through the dust of his ancestors. Batman thought the whole thing was a waste of time.

"Cucumbers I can understand," he said. "There's sense in cucumbers, but poking about for years on end in that historical dustbin – where's the sense in that? Still, if it keeps the Colonel happy there's nae harm, I suppose."

At first I'm sure that Colonel Bogey was as happy as a Rat in a rick. But as he worked his way, year by year, down his family tree, he began to find something nibbling at the roots. Was it possible that the "Bignose curse" they'd laughed at for generations was not just a family joke? Colonel Bogey, Sir Albert, the last of the Bignoses, began to smell a Rat.

It was string that sealed our fate. That's what the Colonel was looking for, poking about in the old kitchen window seat. He needed it to tie up his cucumbers. What he found, under a pile of hats, recipe books and Victorian laundry bills, was a small iron-bound chest.

"Well, well, well, what have we here?" The Colonel hauled it out. "Looks jolly ancient. What the devil was it doing in there?" The chest wasn't locked. With great excitement, he took out and unrolled one of the accounts from the building of Knotty Oak Castle. A small piece of parchment fell out. Colonel Bogey bent down and picked it up.

"How very odd – looks like a poem or something . . . let me see." He held the parchment close to the end of his nose.

". . . Signed by some chap who calls himself . . . can't quite make it out . . . ah yes, Pierre le Drain . . . Well, well, and what does Monsieur le Drain have to say for himself, eh?" The Colonel squinted at the title, spluttered, "Good grief!!'' and sat down heavily in the kitchen chair.

Hours later Batman found Colonel Bogey still sitting in the kitchen chair. He was staring at the Bignose curse, white-faced and mumbling about Rats.

Batman put a blanket around his shoulders and a large brandy in his hand. All that non-sense about witches and Rat-curses – he didn't believe a word of it, but he wasn't going to have the Colonel worried for all the cake in Dundee. The Rats would have to go.

"It's high time we got the wee beasties out of that fountain, by fair means or foul. Dinna ye worry about a thing, Colonel." He pointed at the trusty Bertrund. "By the time we've finished, there'll no be a Rat in the garden."

Batman's first plan was to drop a smoke bomb through one of the holes he'd shot in the fountain. It fizzled and phutted long enough for us to roll it under the terrace along a tunnel we used to raid his larder. Batman and Bertrund were watching from the safety of the pump-house when the smoke bomb went off right under their feet. How we laughed when the pump-house door burst open and they staggered out through the clouds of orange smoke, eyes streaming and coughing fit to burst!

After a few days he tried again, this time with half a dozen ferrets – vicious little things that moved like pink-eyed snakes. They didn't stand a chance. We let them wear themselves out chasing us around the pipes until they were all but tied in knots. Then packs of our biggest rats ambushed them one by one and bundled them out of the fountain. Batman's eyes weren't what they were. "Look out, Bertrund!" he shouted. "Here they come!" and he blasted the lot with his elephant gun.

When weeks went by without a squeak from Batman, we began to believe he'd given up. Looking back, it's hard to believe we could have been so stupid.

We sat around our Stone telling stories of how we'd beaten Batman the Bad and Bertrund the Beast. We boasted of our cunning and felt safe inside our bronze fortress. We paid dearly for the lesson that Rats should never underestimate the ruthlessness of men.

It began with a week of banging and swearing from the pump-house. I could still squeeze through the pipes to the King's head, so I took to spying on him. Batman had a determined look that worried me. I watched him carry in sacks of coal. What was he doing with coal?

Well, Spratt, I thought, he's not going to eat

it, is he? And you won't find out by sitting on your tail!

That night, when I was sure Batman and Bertrund were asleep, I crept down the pipes and under the terrace to the pump-house. The tunnel still smelled strongly of smoke, and when my nose came up against the bomb canister, I knew the enemy were right above my head. It made your whiskers twitch, I can tell you. No turning back – up through a crack in the floorboards. Heart thumping . . . a mixture of smells – dog . . . porridge . . . old socks . . . soot. Snoring from the corner and . . . EEEEEEKKKKKK!

A Monster! Huge glass eyes staring down from the dark, a cavernous black brick mouth – a rusty skyscraper of pipes and valves that might have escaped from a junk yard. The steam pump!

It wasn't a loud squeak but it woke the enemy. There was just time for a quick look at Batman's nest. Workbench and tools, table,

chair, cooker, well-stocked shelves, a bunk –
with Batman and Bertrund blinking at me with
their mouths open. I was off before either of
them was out of bed. Halfway along the tunnel
I heard Batman's army boot bouncing across

the pump-house floor. Back in the safety of my nest, I fell asleep still wondering what Batman was up to.

The smell of smoke woke me early next morning. It was just getting light. When I scrambled to the top of the fountain, black clouds were belching from the pump-house chimney. Steam and curses poured out of the door. The sound of coal shovelling. Hammering. The creak of rusty levers. I heard Batman shout, "Come on, ye great overgrown kettle . . ." There came an angry "Hisssssssssss!" in reply. More hammering and then the hissing stopped . . . CHUG! . . . CHUG! . . . CHUG! CHUG CHUG CHUG!

Batman had started the old steam engine. The pump-house disappeared in clouds of steam out of which came a blackened figure with a crowbar. He jammed it in one of the rusty valves that stuck up from the terrace and heaved. A hundred-odd years of rust does not shift easily.

"Move, you rusty son-of-a—" It moved. Batman fell backwards with a shout. The whole fountain began to shudder. Too late I saw the danger. I tried to warn the tribe but when I reached the pipe I was bowled over by a huge rush of water. Rats were shooting out of the fountain like corks from a bottle. Batman, dashing about in the spray like a madman, was catching Rats in a shrimping net and stuffing them in a sack. Some landed in the pond and found Bertrund waiting as they tried to climb out. A few escaped to the garden. I watched it all from King Neptune's crown and I won't forget it until the day I die. The boiler soon gave out, too late for my friends and family.

Batman spent the rest of the day plugging all the holes in the fountain. He cemented over every crack and cranny Bertrund could find in the terrace. "Well, we've got rid of them at last, Betrund," he said with a grin. "I hope the old king won't be lonely without his wee lodgers. Now, with the help of our little round-up, we can finish the job once and for all." He carried the writhing sack of Rats to an overgrown potting shed in the corner of the garden.

I watched from the king's head until the lights went out in the pump-house. Stiff with cold, I crept down and searched the fountain. It was like an empty tomb. I lay on the Stone and tried to sleep, thinking that things were as bad as they could be. How was I to know that Batman had an even nastier trick up his sleeve.

The idea came from one of Sir Isambard's books that Batman found in the library – *One Man and his Rats*, written by an old rat-catcher called Squizzy Grimes. Mr Grimes spent his life creeping about the sewers of old London, murdering every Rat he could find. It was his favourite method, "What had never been known to fail," that Batman followed to the letter.

About fifty of my friends and relatives were in the sack that he carried to the potting shed. He shook the terrified Rats into a wire cage, covered them with heavy sacks and left them, crammed together in the darkness. Every day he gave them water but never enough. Desperate with thirst and hunger, they had to fight to stay alive. Smaller Rats began to disappear and as weeks went by, there were fewer and fewer in that dreadful cage. After a month, one Rat was left alive. It was Uncle Sharkie – scarred, blind in one eye, completely murderously mad – and a cannibal.

Then the worst part. Batman let him go.

Something Nasty from the Potting Shed

It could only have been a few weeks, but it seemed to take half a lifetime of frantic searching before I found a way out of the fountain. If there hadn't been a store of hazelnuts in the King's beard, I would not be telling you this tale. After a lot of digging and scraping, I managed to squeeze through a crack in the terrace where an old tunnel had collapsed. I found myself right under the garden bench. I looked around. It seemed quiet enough. In front of me two sparrows squabbled over some crisps. I was starving. In the shade of what I took to be a mossy old tree trunk, I edged towards the crisps, nipped out and grabbed one. Cheese and onion! My favourite.

"Oi, you! Clear off! This is our patch."

Sparrows have no manners. I ignored them. Then the sun seemed to go in. Something huge lowered itself towards me. A voice boomed, "Well, well. What have we here?" A great Bignose nose pointed straight at me. Deep-set watery eyes. Colonel Bogey! The enemy! The tree trunk was his old tweed trousers.

"Good grief! A long-tailed field mouse. Haven't seen one in years." He emptied the crisp packet onto the stones in front of me. "There you are, little chap. Eat up if you're hungry." I dived for cover. Halway back along the tunnel, I stopped. Why was I running? If Colonel Bogey didn't think I was a Rat, it was perfectly safe. Back I went and cleared up what the sparrows had left, while the Colonel looked on and smiled.

The weather became very warm, with long

sunny days. I couldn't bear the emptiness inside the fountain, so I spent all my time at the old look-out, watching the garden and sleeping under the stars. I felt safe with the old king. Every day at twelve o'clock on the dot, the Colonel shared his lunch with me. He always seemed pleased to have my company and shooed away the sparrows until I'd finished.

As the summer slipped by without so much as a glimpse of a tail or whisker, desperation for news of my friends drove me out of the fountain to search the garden at night. You can imagine how I felt when I found one of my sisters. We spoke quickly for she seemed nervous, jumping at every sound and shadow. She told me that most of the Rats that had escaped from the flooded fountain had either left the garden or disappeared. Nothing had been seen of those that had been caught by Batman.

"I'm leaving myself tomorrow night," she said, "so we must say goodbye. But before I go, little Spratt, you must promise me that you'll never again leave the fountain after dark. The garden has become very dangerous."

"If it's Batman and Bertrund," I said, "don't worry. I'm very careful and they have to sleep sometime."

She shuddered. "No, Spratt, it's something far worse – something evil that stalks our tracks at night. It seems to know everything about us – all our ways and secrets. Spratt, you must be very careful, you must—" From somewhere not so far away came a low hiss. My sister spun around. She screamed, "Run, Spratt!! Run!!" and disappeared.

I ran. Her terror lent wings to my feet. Whatever it was came crashing after me but I made it to the crack under the bench.

Back in the safety of the fountain, the fear wouldn't leave me. When at last I fell asleep, it curdled my dreams into nightmares. Roaring steam engines galloped after me on pipes that coiled and hissed like snakes. A giant ferret in a kilt shoved me down and down into a bottomless black sack. I must have cried out, for somewhere in the darkness of the garden a voice called back.

"Spratt, my little apprentice, is that you?" The ferret disappeared. I was wide awake. "Come and talk to your Uncle Sharkie."

It was his voice. I knew that, just as I knew that the very sound of it made my hair stand on end. It was without life or feeling, as if Uncle Sharkie had lost his soul. I said nothing and covered my ears until the morning light drove him back to the shadows.

He came every night after that. I watched

him for hours, a darker shape in the darkness, padding round and round on the old stones that edged the pond.

"Come out, little Spratt . . . Come out, little Spratt . . . I saved your life . . . I want it back," chanted the dead voice, and every now and again the moonlight on the pond flashed like a tiny star in his one mad eye.

An Oily Slug

I think eventually loneliness and the fear of Uncle Sharkie would have driven me as mad as he was, but Batman fell off his ladder and changed everything. To tell the truth, he didn't fall – he was thrown off by an electric shock from his hedge-trimmer. Uncle Sharkie had chewed the cable. His leg was broken and the hospital sent him to the Waterloo Home for Old Soldiers to recuperate for a few weeks.

While Batman was out of the way, Rupert Doiley-Pratt, who claimed to be a distant relation of the Colonel's, began to call at the house. Rupert was a fat, oily slug. He said that he wheeled and dealed somewhere in the City, but in fact he worked for the developers Grabbold & Nickett Inc., and had been trying to get his podgy hands on Colonel Bogey's property for years. Once before, Rupert had invited himself to tea. Batman took an instant dislike to him and served up cold tea and stale scones, while Bertrund chewed his umbrella under the settee.

"Good riddance!" said Batman when he'd gone. "I would not trust that one further than I could spit ma sporran. I hope his umbrella doesn't upset Bertrund's stomach."

"Can't say I cared much for the fellow either," agreed the Colonel. "Kept calling me Uncle Albey, and look! The greedy blighter's eaten all the scones."

But the Colonel was old and tired. He was lost without Batman, so when Rupert called again and offered to move in ("Just to lend a hand until your little Scottish chappie is up and about again"), the Colonel agreed.

"Don't you worry about a thing, Uncle Albey," he smarmed. "Just carry on with your books and cucumbers and leave everything to me." It was Rupert's intention that the Colonel should leave everything to him, or at least let him have it for next to nothing.

"I'll wait on the old fool hand and foot for a few days until he's convinced that I'm a thoroughly nice chap, then splish, splash with a drop of petrol and woomph! The tatty old pile will go up like a bloomin' bonfire. A heroic rescue before things get too hot and the old twit will be so grateful he'll let me have what's left of the place for a song." Rupert Doiley-Pratt smiled an oily smile.

Bertrund hadn't left the Colonel's side since Batman was carted off to hospital. At night he slept at the end of his bed and the two of them snored a duet that I could hear from the top of the fountain. So Rupert knew they were asleep when he sneaked downstairs from his bedroom, carrying a large can of petrol.

Rupert was nervous. In the kitchen he put down the can, rested his torch on the dresser and lit a cigarette. "Just a quick fag to calm the old nerves," he said to himself. "Doesn't do to rush these things." Next to the torch he noticed a large box of crisps. "Hmmm, cheese and onion." Rupert liked crisps. He reached into the box.

With Batman and Bertrund out of the way, Uncle Sharkie had taken to raiding the kitchen at night, and it happened that he was in the crisp box helping himself, when a fat finger came and poked him in the ribs. He bit it. Rupert screamed, dropped his cigarette and tipped over the can. He rushed up the stairs to the hall with the huge Rat hanging from his finger. The noise woke Bertrund and his barking woke Colonel Bogey.

"Raiders!" shouted the Colonel, jumping out of bed. "Come on, Bertrund, m'lad!"

Meanwhile, Rupert had shaken himself free of Uncle Sharkie and was hiding behind the settee. By the light of the moon through the stained glass window, he saw Colonel Bogey stride onto the landing in his nightshirt, waving a huge sword. He didn't look old or frail.

"I know you're there, blast it! Come out and show yourselves."

Rupert crouched lower. A spring twanged. Bertrund charged down the stairs and shot under the settee but he didn't find Rupert – he found Uncle Sharkie hiding in the springs.

Bertrund yelped as Uncle Sharkie's great yellow teeth sank into his nose. Claws raked at his eyes. The little dog fell backwards in surprise. Rats don't do this, he thought. But there were no rules for Uncle Sharkie. Bertrund was fighting for his life.

And what a fight! What shrieking and snarling and twanging of springs.

Uncle Sharkie was quick, vicious and mad. Bertrund, old as he was, had the heart of a lion and jaws like a steel trap. The settee bulged and writhed with battle. Colonel Bogey shouted and slashed with his sword. Rupert cringed, lower and lower, expecting at any moment to be sliced like a salami.

How I wish I'd been there to see it all! A sword-swipe slit the settee from stem to stern. Dog and Rat rolled out into the middle of the hall in a tangle of blood and fur. They broke apart then stood and glared at each other, splashed with coloured moonlight from the stained glass window.

Eyes fixed, the two animals began a deadly, slow-footed dance. Round and round in the

pool of colour . . . blue, green, red – black spots of blood in the dust – watching, waiting.

When Uncle Sharkie charged, Bertrund was ready for him and they went at it tooth and claw, no holds barred and devil take the hindmost. Over tables, under chairs from one end of the hall to the other. Scattering ornaments, smashing vases. Suits of armour crashed to the floor. Stuffed birds flew to pieces from their shattered glass cages. It was all too quick for the Colonel. He watched in wonder, shouting, "That's my boy! At him, Bertrund!"

Round the hall and round again. Up the stairs and down again. SNARL! SLASH! SCREECH! CRASH!

Bertrund needed no encouragement and

Uncle Sharkie was mad, so I wouldn't like to guess who would have won if the battle hadn't reached the grand piano.

PLINKITY! PLONKITY! PLUNK! They fought their way across the keys. Uncle Sharkie gripped an ear. Bertrund was clamped to his tail. TWING! TWONG! TWANG! Across the strings, like a hippo dancing on a harp. TWING! TWANG! SNARL! SCREECH! and then CHAARRRAANG!!! One tremendous discord as the heavy piano lid crashed down. The noise quivered on the air, slowly fading to silence.

"Bertrund," whispered the Colonel. "Bertrund old chap, are you all right?" Fearfully he lifted the lid, dreading what he might find. Out shot Uncle Sharkie. He had crossed the hall and disappeared into an old Rathole in the stuffed elephant's foot before Bertrund fell out of the piano, snarling and chewing at the end of Uncle Sharkie's tail. He hadn't realized that the rest of the Rat had gone.

"Good old Bertrund!" cheered the Colonel.

"Come on! We've got him now! Tally Ho!"

He charged the elephant and with one magnificent swipe of his sword, took off the whole leg. In my opinion it's never a good idea to hang around a three-legged elephant, stuffed or unstuffed. A second leg crumpled. The Colonel was too slow to get out of the way and the whole thing toppled over in a cloud of dusty straw and earwigs with him trapped underneath.

By now the fire had crept up the kitchen stairs. A hippopotamus head above the door suddenly burst into flames and that set the tiger

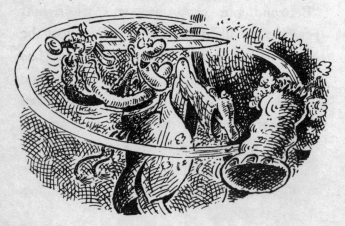

above him burning bright enough to catch the crocodile. His fiery breath spread the flames up from Apache war bonnets to Zulu masks until they were licking at the rafters. In minutes the hall roof was ablaze.

When Rupert dragged the Colonel from under the elephant, the old man was laughing in spite of the pain.

"What a way to go!" he gasped. "Done in by an elephant in me own hall."

The first crash of battle had woken me where I slept on the old king's head. I looked out through his crown and wondered at the noise. I saw the first wisps of smoke blossom into flames. I watched the flames spread across the roof of the hall until the great stained glass window was lit like a banquet of jewels. Then there were sirens, flashing lights, black figures against the burning building – and a smaller black shape, that crept unnoticed from the shadow of the hall doorway as Uncle Sharkie made his escape to the garden.

The Devil and the Deep Blue Sea

Colonel Bogey was taken to join Batman in the Waterloo Home for Old Soldiers. The loss of his old home was a sadness from which he never recovered. Gradually his life faded away while he swopped good memories and bad jokes with his old friend Batman McPile.

The summer turned sour, the days hung heavy and clogged with heat. Great hulks of cloud loomed over the ruined house and garden, purple grey, grumbling with thunder and spiked with lightning. I spent my time curled up in the king's nose, feeling very sorry for myself. When the last few hazelnuts were gone it was starvation or Uncle Sharkie. The Devil or the deep blue sea – not much of a choice.

As it turned out I didn't have to choose – I got both.

It started with the rain – and what rain! Huge single drops at first, each one sounding a different note on the old bronze walls. I lay in my nest listening to the tune get faster and wilder until the whole fountain rang – like a thousand tin drums in a waterfall. Climbing up from the nest, I looked out through the eyes of the king. In all his years I'm sure he'd never seen a storm like this.

Perhaps it rained for days – I couldn't say, for there was little to tell night from day. Anyway, what difference did it make to me? I was alone and frightened with nowhere to go. I missed my family and friends – I even missed Colonel Bogey. Later, when I looked out, it seemed the whole world had turned to water. The fountain was a bronze island floating on a grey sea. Let it rain as much as it likes, I thought. At least I'm warm and dry. I crawled into my nest and fell asleep.

I woke up swimming. The fountain was full of roaring, rushing water. This time it wasn't Batman's steam pump, it was Nickspiddle Spring. For centuries it had run peacefully under great stone slabs, trickled obediently from the pond to the canal. Not any more. The storm had woken it with a vengeance and, like a cork in a volcano, the fountain was in its way.

In a bubbling sneeze I shot out through the king's left nostril. The rain caught me and washed me down through his beard, rolled me along the folds of his cloak like a marble in a gutter. I bounced from Mr Gladstone's head to Queen Victoria's tail and plopped, gasping, into the pond. Crash after crash of thunder rolled overhead. Around me the water boiled and flashed from inky blackness to the brightest day.

Swim, Spratt! Swim for your life! Rain zipped like bullets. Which way? . . . don't know . . . keep swimming . . . tangles of water lilies . . . swim! swim! . . . it's too far! . . . swimming in circles . . . I'm going to drown! I'm going to drown! . . . swim! swim! swim! . . . at last! . . . something solid. The edge· of the pond. I dragged myself onto the stones and lay in a soggy heap, too exhausted to move.

"So you've come to me at last, little Spratt?"

The nightmare wasn't over. It had been waiting at the edge of the pond. I looked up . . . a huge black shape . . . one mad eye – Uncle Sharkie.

Yellow teeth came closer . . . whispering, "I

knew that I only had to wait and the storm would bring you to me. There has to be a last sacrifice to the stones."

He was going to kill me!

"No!" I screamed. "No, Uncle Sharkie. I won't be a proper sacrifice – I'm too small. No . . . Uncle . . . Sharkie . . . please!!!"

Behind him, I saw the fountain lift, its great weight pushed up by the force of Nickspiddle Spring. Water burst from the blocked holes and the fountain gave its last, mad display. Uncle Sharkie hesitated. King Neptune reached up – zigzagged lightning met his trident. Noise! . . . too loud to hear! . . . blue-white flash! . . . boiling! . . . sparks! The King's arm flung downwards. Uncle Sharkie's scream, cut short by the crushing trident.

I remember clinging to something and being whirled around and around in a cauldron of mud, stones and bubbles. A great surge of water as the old walls gave way. Rushing along in darkness and then a long time of nothingness.

It was cold. There was a chattering noise in a grey fog. Teeth don't chatter if you're dead, I thought, so I must be alive. At the time it didn't matter. Later it seemed possible to open one eye. The storm was over. I was drifting between banks of boats and barges. Their colours sparkled in the clear morning. For a while it was enough to float through this new world with the rising sun warm on my back. Perhaps being alive wasn't so bad, but how? – why? – what was it that had saved my life? I drifted, eyes shut, rocked gently by the water. Eventually I managed to lift my head, not sure that anything else would move. It was an odd-looking life raft – like a lumpy old sofa, with matted black fur. It reminded me of . . . I sat up, the raft rolled slightly – great yellow teeth broke the surface – a soft hiss of escaping air. Oh, horrors!! Staring straight at me . . . ONE MAD, DEAD, BLACK EYE!!!

I found I could move very quickly. I was into the water, paddling frantically for the nearest

barge. The barge wasn't far but it was too far for me. My paddling got slower and slower as I sank beneath the waves.

"Goodbye, world," I bubbled, as the bright surface slipped away – not very original, but you don't make long speeches when you're drowning. Down . . . down . . . I watched my last breath spiral lazily upwards. Down . . . down . . . down . . . And then – a miracle. Up . . . up . . . up – something whisked me up in a splashing, flashing arc through the bright morning and plonked me sprawling onto the deck of the barge like a landed fish.

What next? I was washed up, tossed up, tail up and twisted. It felt like I'd spent a week wrestling an elephant in a tumble dryer. So I'll just lie here, I thought, on this nice warm deck and wait and see.

The sun lifted clear into a blue sky. Downstream, Uncle Sharkie's body drifted slowly out of sight.

"Oh, you poor dear," said a voice. "You look

like a drowned Rat . . . Never mind . . . nobody's perfect . . . Let's get you into the warm." I was picked up very gently, carried into the barge and put in a shoe-box by the stove – as if it were something the owner of the voice did every day. "So nice to have company at last . . . wasn't it lucky I remembered the shrimping net in my handbag? . . . Can I offer you a potato crisp? Goodness me, I haven't introduced myself. My name is Miss Jezabella Jones."

A Hot Rock Shock

At the moment the fountain was struck by lightning, Colonel Bogey, Sir Albert, the last of the Bignoses, died peacefully in his sleep at the Waterloo Home for Old Soldiers. He left everything he had to Batman McPile.

Batman let Rupert Doiley-Pratt have the house and garden. It meant nothing to him any more. He and Bertrund went to have a last look through the gates.

"Nothing but a burnt-out ruin in a muddy wee puddle." The garden, the fountain and the spirit of the place had all been washed away.

But to Rupert it meant a couple of Porsches and a villa in the South of France.

"Just have to clear the site and sell it for loads of jolly old money."

It only took a few days to bulldoze the house and walls.

"We'll finish tomorrow – no problem," said the foreman. In the morning, he rang Rupert's office with a problem.

"We can't shift it," he said. "When the crane driver bashed it, it broke his big iron ball. He's not well pleased, I can tell you. We tried blowing it up, but it wouldn't budge an inch."

Rupert drove to the site, trying to remember if he'd ever seen a long pointed stone in the garden. He picked his way through the rubble towards a small group of men. They let him through. There it was, yellow-grey, slightly curved – and over two metres tall.

"I've never come across anything like it," said the foreman . . . "And that's not all – just you put your 'and on it."

Nervously, Rupert touched the stone. "Ouch! It's hot!!" he squealed.

"Right!" agreed the foreman. "But the really odd thing, Mr Doiley-Pratt, is that the bloomin' thing's still growing."

On a Monday morning a couple of days later, about half a mile away in another part of the city, old Harry Salway, gravedigger and odd job man, was sitting in a church porch waiting for the rain to ease off. He blew on the tea from his flask and read the headlines of his local paper. HOT ROCK SHOCK! it said. GROWING MYSTERY ON BUILDING SITE. The story interested Harry because he'd grown up in one of the back-to-backs called Knotty Oak Villas. As a boy his grandfather had worked in the garden of the big house and he used to frighten young Harry with stories of the mad Bignoses and the Devil's Stone under the fountain. Harry chuckled at the memory as he folded his paper.

"What a load of old nonsense." He packed away his flask, picked up his tools and made his way through a maze of mossy gravestones. Today he had to finish clearing the brambles around the old cross at the back of the church. The rain had stopped and the sun was out. A blackbird sang from the top of a yew tree. Perhaps the weather's on the change again, thought Harry as he rounded the corner of the tower. He stopped. He gasped . . .

"Great Gawd Almighty!! . . . What's happened to the Parson's Nose?" The Parson's Nose was a small, pointed stone that stood at the base of the cross, said to be even older than the cross itself. Last week it had been almost covered by brambles. It wasn't covered now, it was more than two metres tall – and steaming. For a long time Harry just stared, then he fetched his bicycle from the tool shed and hurried out of the churchyard.

"Can't it wait, Harry?" said the vicar when he opened the door. "I'm collecting jumble for the church this morning." Harry said that he didn't think it could wait and reluctantly the vicar followed him back to the churchyard. When he saw what had happened to the Parson's Nose the vicar forgot the jumble.

"I've never seen anything like it, Harry. It must be at least two metres tall. Stones don't just grow like mushrooms, do they? Oh dear me, I wonder if we ought to send for the Bishop."

Harry looked long and hard at the stone. It gave him a very uneasy feeling. He was a careful man and not to be hurried. He thought about his grandfather's stories and about an identical stone growing on a building site not a kilometre away. Finally, he said, "Tell me, Vicar, does the devil always have two horns?"

The vicar didn't know what to say. He could see Harry wasn't joking.

"Er . . . well, Harry. Er . . . so we've always been led to believe."

"Well, I could be wrong, Vicar," said Harry, putting on his bicycle clips, "but I reckon the quicker you send for the Bishop, the better."

Miss Jezabella Jones

Miss Jezabella Jones seemed to know a thing or two about Rats. While I was drying out by the stove, she began reaching down bottles and jars from her kitchen shelves, tipping a splish of this and a splosh of that into a big black pot. When it came to the boil, she stirred the brew with the end of an old hockey stick, humming all the while. It smelled like boiled compost.

"Eat it all up," she hummed, plonking a saucer of green sludge under my nose. "You'll feel like a new Rat." I sniffed it.

Yuck!! But I was hungry and anyway it takes a lot to poison a Knotty Oak Rat, so I ate the lot. I remember thinking Hmmmm, not bad, when someone turned off the world. Next morning I woke tucked up in my box, feeling like a new Rat.

All morning, Miss Jones bustled about the barge chatting away like an old friend. I didn't know what to make of her. You must remember, she was the first lady member of your tribe I had met – for all I knew they were *all* as dotty as dormice. Later, she dragged an old bicycle from among the plants on the barge roof.

"Make yourself at home," she called. "I'm just popping out for a spell." I could hear her laughing all down the towpath.

So I made myself at home – and what a home it was. Draped in curtains with painted stars, lined with old books and overgrown with flowery cushions. In one corner was her hockey stick, shrimping net, a banjo, a pogo-stick, a

broom and a large stuffed eel. Hanging from a rail, above a poster of an odd-looking wrestler, was an assortment of false beards, a catapult, a judge's wig, Doc Marten boots, a dead lizard and a live bat. There were bits and bones from every corner of time and place. Plants sprouted from painted pots, or hung drying in bunches like an upside-down garden. In the middle of it all, dangling from the ceiling like a stuffed hippo, was a large armchair. It swung gently to and fro with the barge. When I climbed up for a swing I found something hard and round under the cushions. It was a crystal ball. There was more to Miss Jezabella Jones than met the eye.

She rattled back about an hour later, a huge box of potato crisps across her handlebars, her handbag bulging and a newspaper stuck like a flag amongst the flowers of her hat.

"Just a few things I think we might be needing." She put the box of crisps under the small table and began unpacking her handbag. Mixed with the usual groceries was a string of garlic, a bag of acorns, toadstools of all shapes and colours, and goodness knows what she'd picked from the hedgerows. If you're wondering how all of this could fit into a handbag, don't ask me.

"I think that's the lot," she said, peering into the bag. "Hang on – not quite." Out came half a dozen bottles of Newcastle Brown Ale and some Jaffa cakes. "They're my favourite," she said, opening the packet. "Try one."

I have to admit that I've since become very fond of Jaffa cakes. Later I had another for my tea while Miss Jones finished the lot *and* washed down four packets of crisps with a bottle of Newcastle Brown. She belched politely. "You look as if you could do with a hand." I was struggling to get into a packet of crisps. She squeezed the bag until it popped open, picked me up by the tail and, with a "*Bon appétit*," dumped me head-first into the crisps. "Salt?" she enquired, and tipped a little blue packet over my head. Then she shook me about in the bag, roaring with laughter. Oh yes, I thought. Very funny, I must say.

I spent the evening sulking in the bottom of my crisp bag. Miss Jones was too busy to notice. After tea she had sat reading the newspaper with her boots up on the stove. She had just finished her second bottle of Newcastle

Brown when suddenly she was on her feet, shouting.

"Lor' lumme!! I knew it! The old boy's a goner!!" In no time the black pot was back on the stove and the day's collection, together with half the barge, seemed to have disappeared into it. Brown ale, packets of tea, string, a box of matches, bits of bones and bunches of berries – all went in.

She was still at it, hunched over some ancient recipe, when I crawled into my shoe box. The black pot grumbled to itself on the stove. I thought, if that's breakfast, I think I'll give it a miss. Some time later I was woken by Miss Jones chasing the bat around the barge with her shrimping net.

There wasn't any breakfast. I found Miss Jones swinging in her armchair, staring into her crystal ball.

"Cooee!" she called. "Don't mind me, just help yourself to whatever you want." Now I ask you, would any of your tribe tell a Rat to help themselves unless they were completely dotty? Well, that's OK by me, I thought. If she's happy to share her barge with a small homeless Rat, why should I complain? I popped to the kitchen and chewed my way into a packet of digestive biscuits.

It seemed a good idea to spend the morning exploring the barge. I found a couple of bolt holes that would come in very handy if the unpredictable Miss Jones should change her mind about Rats.

In the afternoon I tidied my shoe box. I don't know about you, but I've always found chewed newspaper the best thing for a nest, so I climbed into the rubbish bin to find the paper that Miss Jones had thrown away. I'd chewed a nice pile of small pieces when something about the photograph I was nibbling caught my eye. It was Colonel Bogey! Much younger and in uniform, but there was no mistaking that nose. I couldn't think why the Colonel's picture should be in the paper. Could it be that my old friend and enemy had never recovered from the elephant? Was the last of the Bignoses even now pushing up the graveyard roses?

I had a lot to think about, and so, it seemed did Miss Jones. When she wasn't throwing things into her black pot, she was staring into her crystal ball.

This went on for three days and all the while the grumbles, whistles and shrieks from the black pot grew louder, until I could hardly sleep at night. When she lifted the lid on the third morning, Miss Jezabella Jones got quite excited.

"Yes! Yes! Almost ready – just needs a little more time," and she threw in an alarm clock! Completely off her trolley, I thought.

For the rest of the day, Miss Jones couldn't sit still. At five o'clock the alarm clock went off. She jumped out of her chair, grabbed her bicycle and pedalled off without a word. She wasn't long. I was just nibbling the last digestive biscuit when she came tearing back down the towpath. Miss Jezabella Jones was going like a train, a newspaper under her arm, her hair, usually tucked carefully under her hat, flying wildly in the wind – it was bright red. She leapt from the bike to the barge. The bike carried on and leapt into the canal.

"Hell, spell and spit!!" she shouted. "He's on the move."

Miss Jones was in a hurry. She began piling wood into the stove until the noise from the pot made my ears ring.

"Stand back," she ordered. Lifting the lid, she threw in the bag of acorns and held on tight. The black pot jumped off the stove and bounced around the little kitchen like a bucking bronco, with Miss Jones hanging on like a limpet. Acorns pinged about inside like mega popcorn.

There was a flash and a bang as the lid blew off. I'm not daft – I took cover in my shoe box. When I looked out, the smoke had cleared and Miss Jones was sitting on the floor still holding the pot, face black, hat gone and hair a-fright. When she smiled, her teeth looked very white.

"I think they're done," she said. Miss Jones picked a bright red acorn from the bottom of the pot and held it up. It glowed between her fingers like a red hot coal. She seemed pleased.

"Done to a turn." She tipped the lot into her handbag. "And now we're as ready as we'll ever be." Cramming her hat onto her wild red hair, she said, "Good night," climbed into her chair and immediately began to snore.

Take the Devil by
the Horns

Putt . . . Putt . . . Putt . . . woke me very
early in the morning.

Oh no! I thought. The pot's back on the
boil. But it wasn't the pot, it was the barge's
engine – we were on the move.

I'll never forget those first few hours of
travelling by canal. For a Rat that had only
travelled in tales, it was all I could have dreamed.
Cows, trees and farms glided by in the early
mist, as if the barge stood still while the whole
world revolved slowly beneath it. I sat like a
small Ratty figurehead and watched the water

slide and crumple under the bows.

Funny, I thought. I've never noticed the barge's name. It rippled back at me from the flat surface. I spelt it out: L-L-E-P-S-T-A-R Llepstar? What sort of name was that? Then it hit me – it was a reflection. R-A-T-S-P-E-L-L. Her barge was called *Ratspell*!

I had to think but my head wouldn't stop spinning. Who would call their barge *Ratspell*? Someone unpredictable, someone who boiled mad brews in a black pot – someone with wild red hair. For a long time I stared down into the water. It was unbelievable, it made my tail stand on end, but I had to find out.

She was standing at the tiller when she saw me scuttling slowly along the roof towards her, so we were on the same level when I looked straight into those eyes for the first time. One was sea green, the other sky blue and they seemed to scoop the brain right out of my skull – Nell the Spell.

"Well, Spratt," said Nell the Spell, "I see you've found me out at last. You certainly took your time. I was beginning to wonder if it was worth my while fishing you out of the canal."

I was beginning to wonder if I should jump back in. Sharing a barge with dotty Miss Jones was one thing, being shanghaied by an unpredictable, goodness-knows-how-old mythological witch was something else. But before I could do anything I was whisked from the roof and pinned to the deck, with one of Nell's boots firmly on my tail. She took a newspaper from her handbag and placed it in front of me. The photographs of the two rocks were almost identical. One was being examined by a worried-looking vicar.

"DOUBLE TROUBLE", ran the headline. "VICAR IN SECOND HOT ROCK SHOCK!"

Nell the Spell bent down and looked me in the eye.

"I need your help, Spratt. If I can't put Old Nick into reverse, he'll have the poor old vicar's church for a top hat." She straightened up. "We've got another hour or so before we reach Knotty Oak, so just you sit there, young Spratt, and I'll tell you a story."

Nell would have made a good storyteller. She told me that, like the rest of the gods of the old world, Old Nick should have faded back to the earth long ago. But he was a stubborn, bad-tempered old god and in no hurry to fade away. He was kept in his place by the spell of oak, stone and spring, with Nell as his guardian.

There he should have stayed while his power drained slowly away and he turned to stone.

"You can't begin to imagine how boring it is sitting in a draughty old tree for centuries on end," said Nell. "I kept my hand in with the odd spell for the villagers, but by the time that awful Burt Bignose came along I'd had enough, I can tell you." She let Sir Burt break the spell of wood, stone and water and replaced it with the Bignose curse.

"Yes, I know it was very irresponsible but it was a dead-end job. I was only a few centuries old and I'd always wanted a career that involved travelling or the theatre. Anyway, I was sure that by the time the last Bignose was pushing up roses, Old Nick would have turned to stone long ago. And that, young Spratt, is where you come in," said Nell. She had to have a Knotty Oak Rat to help reverse the curse. "It should have been your Uncle Sharkie," she sighed.

Apparently, Nell had had a Rat as a travelling companion for years, ever since her last cat got bored with the theatre and ran off to sea as ship's cat to Blackbeard the pirate.

"I found I much preferred Rats," said Nell, "and Sharkie was the brightest of the lot. When it looked as if the Colonel would be the last of his line, Sharkie agreed to stay in the garden to keep an eye on things. In fact, I was on my way to Knotty Oak when the two of you came floating by."

I was so bound up with Nell's story that I hadn't noticed the country had given way to the town. The high-rise blocks looked familiar, but I recognized nothing of my old home when we moored alongside the rubble of the old garden walls. Rat-Rot Hall, our small, safe world, had gone for ever. Now it was a swamp of mud, criss-crossed with bulldozer tracks.

In the middle of the site, where the fountain must have been, was a square of tall fencing. I hadn't expected the banner, "HOT ROCK SENSATION – TICKETS £5", or the coloured

lights, or the long queue of sightseers. And wasn't that Rupert Doiley-Pratt taking the money at the turnstile?

"I think we're a little early," said Nell. "So while we're waiting, let me explain Plan A."

Plan A was simple enough. To reverse the curse you cast the same spell backwards. The more bits of old spell you threw in, the better your chances of making it work.

"So as it's a Knotty Oak Rat curse, I need a Knotty Oak Rat." Nell looked around at the flattened garden walls. "Thank goodness we still have the stones. We're a bit short on springs so I'll use my pogo-stick. I prefer it to my broom anyway." She patted her handbag and winked. "Our special acorns are ready – and we've got this . . ."

Nell placed a small stony splinter in front of me. It was yellow-grey and pulsed with a light of its own. Although I'd never seen it before I knew it like the back of my paw. How many times had I sat in that shape and told tales from the top of the Stone? It was the splinter from the Devil's Horn.

"It doesn't look much, does it?" said Nell. "But it's the key to the curse. While we have it, we hold much of Old Nick's power and he can only grow very slowly." She crossed her fingers. "Let's hope Plan A works, young Spratt, because if we have to use Plan B, we must give the old devil back his splinter."

We waited on the barge until the puddles on the deserted site shone pink in the setting sun.

Nell the Spell had everything we needed stowed in her handbag. When the orange rim of the sun disappeared behind the tower blocks, Nell said,

"Well, this is it, young Spratt! Time to take the Devil by the horns."

A Merry-go-Round

I picked up the Devil's splinter. Nell picked me up and put me with the flowers in her hat.

We made our way between the puddles towards the coloured lights. I felt very nervous. From where I sat on Nell's hat, I could just see the tip of the horn over the fencing. Wisps of steam rose in the cooling air. As we got closer, a figure came out of the gate. He waved us away.

"Clear off! The show's over for today. I'm locking up."

Nell the Spell smiled sweetly.

"Oh, what a pity! Wouldn't it be possible to let me in just for a quick peep? I have come rather a long way."

"No, it bloomin' well wouldn't!" squealed the oily Rupert. "Where would I be if I let every overdressed, hippy oik come and go as they pleased?"

He took out his keys and locked the gate.

"Now shove off."

Nell was still smiling as she took her hockey stick out of her handbag. "If you don't let me in, Mr Doiley-Pratt, I shall change you into a slug."

"Oh, really?" laughed Rupert. "Haw! Haw! Haw! A slug, eh? That's awfully good. Some sort of witch are you? Haw! Haw! Haw!"

"Yes," said Nell, and she waved her hockey stick. There wasn't a bang – more a watery sort of "Sploop!!" Rupert disappeared and in the mud, next to his keys, was a large, surprised-looking slug. It doesn't pay to argue with Nell the Spell. She gave another wave of her hockey stick and the gate swung open.

Getting onto the Stone wasn't easy. It had grown so much that Nell couldn't quite reach and I had to scramble up the last bit, carrying the splinter. My legs shook with fright, just like the time I climbed the Stone to tell my first tale. But the view from the top was very different. No fountain with rows of friendly faces – instead, I looked down on a muddy building site, hemmed around with the lights of tall buildings. I shivered in spite of the warmth of the splinter.

If Nell was nervous she didn't show it.

"Righty ho, Spratt! You know what to do. Here we go!"

Handbag on her arm, hockey stick in her hand, she began bouncing backwards on her pogo stick, slowly round the Devil's Horn.

"Just getting the feel of it!" she called. "Hang on!" She was off, faster and faster until she was whirling around like a giant catherine wheel.

"noitan imile tar ot demooD. . . !!"

When Nell let rip with the last words of the backward curse I felt the Devil's Horn lurch under me – like something jolted from sleep. What a noise it made!

The battle was on. Blue sparks snaked between the horn and the whirring witch. Nell was a streak of colour under the coloured lights

– a mad funfair merry-go-round. The Devil's Horn vibrated and grew hot under my feet with the power of the spell. It was beginning to move! Yes – it was going down. No – it was coming up again. The first acorn hit it square in the middle BLAM! A flash – like a small hand grenade.

Down went the horn . . . it shuddered . . . up again. Another acorn BLAM! down again . . . up again . . . down again – like a flea in a fit. Nell's backward chanting was getting louder and more desperate . . .

". . . noitareneg yreve morf enO!!"

Acorns whizzed and banged. Sparks flew and I clung on in terror. Anyone looking down from the buildings must have wondered at the firework display around the Stone. With her last acorn, Nell reached the beginning of the curse.

". . . noitallepskcalb, llepsstraps, – LLEPS-TAR!!!"

She gave the Devil's Horn a great whack

with her hockey stick. The blast blew her off course and sent her crashing into the wooden fencing. A deep, rumbling groan shook the horn. I felt myself going down – and down – and down.

"She's done it! She's done it!" I squeaked, hopping about on the Stone. "Yippee!!" And then it stopped.

I held my breath – waiting. Slowly the Devil's Stone began to rise again.

"Hell, spell, spit in spam!!" screamed Nell. "He's off again, Spratt! We'll have to do it. Plan B . . . Give him back his splinter."

It doesn't pay to argue with Nell the Spell. I dropped the splinter into place and jumped back. It fizzed and flashed until it was as if the mark of Burt Bignose's axe had never been. Before I had a chance to wonder what might happen next, the Devil's Horn began shooting upwards and I fell off. Nell the Spell was back on her pogo-stick. She caught me as she bounced past and stuck me in her hat, shouting,

"Hang on, Spratt!"

We cleared the wooden fence and were off across the wrecked garden like a giant kangaroo, over the rubble of the house – the old gates, still standing. Nell didn't even slow down and we cleared the gates by a couple of metres. I hung on and looked back at all that was left of my old life. Through the twisted wrought iron gates I could see the Devil's Horn already pushing up through the banner, dragging the coloured lights towards the stars.

What a ride! Here was I, a small rodent that had never seen a city, perched on a mad witch's hat, flying past shops, lights, cars and people like a Rat out of hell.

"It'll come up a kilometre or so due west of the centre of the horns," panted Nell as we cleared a double decker bus.

"We haven't got much time."

Boing! . . . Boing! . . . Boing! . . . We were bouncing from roof to roof up a traffic-jammed one way street. There were shouts, breaking glass, blaring horns. People were running out of buildings, staring at the pavement, pointing at the sky – pointing at us. Below the noise and all around I could feel a deep rumble, like an approaching earthquake. In front of us a tall building disappeared into the darkness – then another, and another, their lights going out as if at a flick of a switch. We bounced through red lights, between buses, over cars.

What will come up? I wondered. Where are we going?

Nell the Spell bounced madly onwards.

"We should see it," she gasped, "end of the next street!"

As we passed the last building, everything went dark except for the newest, tallest, most expensive office block in the whole city.

"There!" said Nell. In front of us, a great wall of glass lit the darkness like a Christmas tree. At the top, almost in the clouds, huge red neon letters flashed the company's name – it was the head office of Grabbold & Nickett.

All was not well at Grabbold & Nickett's. People scrambled in panic through the doors, they stood in the street gaping at the quaking building, they leapt out of the way of a flying witch with a Rat on her hat.

With one bound we were through the doors and into the reception hall, amid dust, noise and breaking glass. Chandeliers swayed and plaster fell on potted palms. The lift doors banged and buckled, as if a giant fist was trying to batter its way out.

"It's coming up the lift shaft," shouted Nell. "We must get to the roof!"

Round and round, up the stairs a flight at a time, I could hear whatever it was crashing up behind us. When we burst through the doors to the roof, Nell collapsed in a heap.

"Must sit down . . . get my breath back . . . not the witch I was."

At any other time, I might have enjoyed the view from the roof. Above us "Grabbold & Nickett" flashed off and on, while below in the darkness, lines of traffic crawled like yellow-eyed ants. Westwards, beyond the blacked out city, a streak of pink showed the last of the sun. It was when I looked towards the east that my heart almost stopped. Above the buildings, curving away from a rising moon – two great yellow-grey horns.

Whatever it was crashing up through the lift-shaft was getting closer. Nell was poking about in her handbag.

"Now, if I can only find the salt . . ." Salt?! I thought, SALT?!! . . . Something unbelievably horrible was coming to get us. What was she going to do? Offer it a snack?! I began jumping up and down in fear and fury.

What in the world was it?

Nell picked me from her hat and held me out in front of her. Witch or no witch I faced her, teeth chattering with anger. She laughed.

"Of course . . . poor old Spratt . . . I forgot to explain Plan B. Well, it's simple enough – any child could tell you.

Of the potions and spells
To be rid of the Devil
Nine thousand times ninety will fail.
The only sure way
You can do for Old Nick
Is to sprinkle some salt on his tail."

So, it was the Devil's tail that was battering its way up the lift-shaft and we were going to stop it with an old children's rhyme and a few grains of salt – I had never heard anything so unbelievably stupid in my life.

Nell the Spell stood at the centre of the roof – a small salt-cellar in one hand – waiting to sprinkle salt on the Devil's tail. I don't believe we're doing this, I thought. We might as well try and stop an express train with a pea shooter! We waited – the huge flashing letters turning the roof from darkness to an eerie red, the whole building rocking like a tree in a gale. The end was nearly nigh.

"Ready?" hissed Nell. I wasn't, but what

difference did that make? I crouched amongst the flowers of her hat with my eyes tight shut.

"CRASH!" The devil's tail burst through the roof of the lift-shaft like a super-charged rhinoceros. We were thrown across the roof and Nell's precious salt went sailing over the edge.

"The salt!" she screamed. "We've lost the salt!"

Free of the lift shaft, the Devil's tail writhed and twisted above us like a huge, black, arrow-headed snake, its scales glittered purple-green in the moonlight, its glowing red tip trailing sparks across the night sky. I stared in fascinated horror as it smashed into the neon letters. Nell didn't seem to notice, she stared in the direction of the salt and whispered something – it sounded like "crisps." And then she was shouting "CRISPS!!" and rummaging desperately in her bag.

"Ah ha!" She ripped open the bag and held up something small and blue.

"Come on!" Then we were climbing the framework that held up the swaying letters, ignoring sparks and flying glass. Twice the Devil's tail missed us by inches, but up we went to the very top of the letter "N".

"Time to be a hero, Spratt. If this works, you'll certainly have a tale to tell. If it doesn't – you won't!" Nell handed me the small blue packet, then holding on with one hand she held me out as far as she could with the other.

Dangling above a world that seemed very far away, I felt quite calm. I remember the wind in my whiskers and the strong smell of burning sulphur and the two great horns looming in the distance. Huge and dangerous. What could an old witch and a small rat hope to do against something as monstrous as the Devil? What if it. . . ?

No more time to think – the end of the huge tail was rushing towards us. I ripped the blue packet with my teeth . . . nearer . . . nearer . . . Then Nell screamed, "Now, Spratt!! Now!!!"

I threw the salt.

There was a huge flash and I felt the heat from the tail as it lashed the lettering beside us. It lifted and shook the building like a terrier with a rat. But my eyes were full of salt, and I couldn't see a thing as Nell scrambled back down. I must have missed, I thought miserably.

We crouched in the corner of the roof under a hail of twisted metal and glass as the Devil began to shake Grabbold and Nickett to pieces. Nell said nothing but never took her eyes off the end of the thrashing tail.

Well, I thought, it doesn't look as if I'm going to die quietly in my nest of old age. At least we're going out with a bang.

But now comes the twist at the end of the tale. When I'd rubbed the salt from my eyes the tail looked just as dangerous, and thrashed about just as wildly – so was it my imagination that some of the spark had gone out of the tail's end? Had the blue-green scales just a little less lustre? I was sure that Nell was thinking the same – I could feel her trembling with excitement through the flowers of her hat. Minutes ticked by. Slowly, very slowly but surely the life began to drain from the Devil's tail. From the tip, a stony greyness spread downwards. It aged – cracked and shrivelled before our eyes to a thing with no more power than a church gargoyle. It began to slide back down the lift shaft and as it sank into the earth a deep, sad groan rumbled beneath the city like subterranean thunder.

"We've done it," whispered Nell, then she grabbed me from her hat and threw me in the air, shouting,

"HELL, SPELL, SPIT and SPAM! We've done it Spratt! We've put Old Nick back where he belongs! We've reversed the Bignose curse!"

We sat on the edge of the roof, Nell the Spell and I – dangling our feet in the air and sharing the packet of crisps. They weren't the same

without salt but we couldn't have cared less.
Nell fished a thermos flask from her bottomless
handbag and poured hot, green sludge into a
cup. She put it down beside me.

"Have some soup." I didn't argue . . . no
need to tell you why.

We watched in silence as the two great horns
sank slowly in the east. I thought about my

family, of Uncle Sharkie, the Bignoses and my life as it had been and I felt very grateful that I had survived to tell my tale.

When the very last tip of the Devil's horns had disappeared behind the roofs of the city, Nell turned to me with a wink from her sea green eye.

"My dear Spratt. What a day! What a Ding-dong-do-down-the-Devilley-day!" She began to pack away the soup. "And now that we've saved the world – what shall we do tomorrow?"

There was no need for an answer. Move a mountain? Sail the barge to the moon? Make pigs fly?

Wherever or whatever – she knew I'd be happy just to be there.

"Righty ho!" she said, pulling something like a huge, multicoloured bat from her handbag. "Then it's a quick flap back to the barge – Jaffa cakes and brown ale all round, and in the morning we'll see just where in the world the wind will take us."

With that she stuck me back in her hat, grabbed hold of her multicoloured wingamagig, and with a cheerie, "Have you ever been hang-gliding before?" she jumped off the roof.

THE END

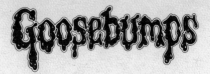

by R.L. Stine

Reader beware, you're in for a scare!

These terrifying tales will send shivers up your spine . . .

Available now:

Look out for:

HIPPO ANIMAL STORIES

If you like animals, then you'll love
Hippo Animal Stories!

Look out for:

Animal Rescue by Bette Paul

Tessa finds life in the country *so* different from life in
the town. Will she ever be accepted? But everything
changes when she meets Nora and Ned who run the
village animal sanctuary, and becomes involved in a
struggle to save the badgers of Delves Wood
from destruction . . .

Thunderfoot by Deborah van der Beek

Mel Whitby has always loved horses, and when she
comes across an enormous but neglected horse in a
railway field, she desperately wants to take care of it.
But little does she know that taking care of
Thunderfoot will change her life forever . . .

A Foxcub Named Freedom
by Brenda Jobling

A vixen lies seriously injured in the undergrowth. Her
young son comes to her for comfort and warmth. The
cub wants to help his mother to safety, but it is
impossible. The vixen, sensing danger, nudges him
away, caring nothing for herself – only for
his freedom . . .

Robert Swindells

"Faithful, fearless, full of fun,
Winter, summer, rain or sun,
One for five, and five for one –
THE OUTFIT!"

*Meet The Outfit—Jillo, Titch, Mickey and Shaz. Share in
their adventures as they fearlessly investigate any mystery,
and injustice, that comes their way . . .*

Move over, Famous Five, The Outfit are here!

The Secret of Weeping Wood

The Outfit are determined to discover the truth about the
eerie crying, coming from scary Weeping Wood. Is the
wood really haunted?

We Didn't Mean To, Honest!

The marriage of creepy Kenneth Kilchaffinch to snooty
Prunella could mean that Froglet Pond, and all its
wildlife, will be destroyed. So it's up to The Outfit to
make sure the marriage is off . . . But how?

Kidnap at Denton Farm

Farmer Denton's new wind turbine causes a protest
meeting in Lenton, and The Outfit find themselves in
the thick of it. But a *kidnap* is something they didn't
bargain for . . .

The Ghosts of Givenham Keep

What is going on at spooky Givenham Keep? It can't be
haunted, can it? The Outfit are just about to find out . . .

Our favourite Babysitters are detectives too! Don't miss the new series of Babysitters Club Mysteries:

Available now:

No 1: Stacey and the Missing Ring
When Stacey's accused of stealing a valuable ring from a new family she's been sitting for, she's devastated – Stacey is *not* a thief!

No 2: Beware, Dawn!
Just *who* is the mysterious "Mr X" who's been sending threatening notes to Dawn and phoning her while she's babysitting, *alone*?

No 3: Mallory and the Ghost Cat
Mallory thinks she's solved the mystery of the spooky cat cries coming from the Craine's attic. But Mallory can *still* hear crying. Will Mallory find the *real* ghost of a cat this time?

No 4: Kristy and the Missing Child
When little Jake Kuhn goes missing, Kristy can't stop thinking about it. Kristy makes up her mind. She *must* find Jake Kuhn . . . wherever he is!

No 5: Mary Anne and the Secret in the Attic
Mary Anne is curious about her mother, who died when she was just a baby. Whilst rooting around in her creepy old attic Mary Anne comes across a secret she never knew . . .

Look out for:

No 6: The Mystery at Claudia's House
No 7: Dawn and the Disappearing Dogs
No 8: Jessi and the Jewel Thieves
No 9: Kristy and the Haunted Mansion
No 10: Stacey and the Mystery Money

The Babysitters Club

Need a babysitter? Then call the Babysitters Club. Kristy Thomas and her friends are all experienced sitters. They can tackle any job from rampaging toddlers to a pandemonium of pets. To find out all about them, read on!

GREEN WATCH by Anthony Masters

BATTLE FOR THE BADGERS
Tim's been sent to stay with his weird Uncle Seb and his two kids, Flower and Brian, who run Green Watch – an environmental pressure group. At first Tim thinks they're a bunch of cranks – but soon he finds himself battling to save badgers from extermination . . .

SAD SONG OF THE WHALE
Tim leaps at the chance to join Green Watch on an anti-whaling expedition. But soon, he and the other members of Green Watch, find themselves shipwrecked and fighting for their lives . . .

DOLPHIN'S REVENGE
The members of Green Watch are convinced that Sam Jefferson is mistreating his dolphins – but how can they prove it? Not only that, but they must save Loner, a wild dolphin, from captivity . . .

MONSTERS ON THE BEACH
The Green Watch team is called to investigate a suspected radiation leak. Teddy McCormack claims to have seen mutated crabs and sea-plants, but there's no proof, and Green Watch don't know whether he's crazy or there's been a cover-up . . .

GORILLA MOUNTAIN
Tim, Brian and Flower fly to Africa to meet the Bests, who are protecting gorillas from poachers. But they are ambushed and Alison Best is kidnapped. It is up to them to rescue her *and* save the gorillas . . .

SPIRIT OF THE CONDOR
Green Watch has gone to California on a surfing holiday – but not for long! Someone is trying to kill the Californian Condor, the bird cherished by an Indian tribe – the Daiku – and without which the tribe will die. Green Watch must struggle to save both the Condor and the Daiku . . .

Hippo Fantasy

Lose yourself in a whole new world, a world where anything is possible – from wizards and dragons, to time travel and new civilizations ... Gripping, thrilling, scary and funny by turns, these Hippo Fantasy titles will hold you captivated to the very last page.

The Night of Wishes
Michael Ende (author of *The Neverending Story*)

It's New Year's Eve, and Beelzebub Preposteror, sorceror and evil-doer, has only seven hours to complete his annual share of villainous deeds and *completely destroy the world!*

Rowan of Rin
Emily Rodda

The witch Sheba has made a mysterious prophecy, which is like a riddle. A riddle Rowan must solve if he is to find out the secret of the mountain and save Rin from disaster ...

The Wednesday Wizard
Sherryl Jordan

Denzil, humble apprentice to the wizard Valvasor, is in a real pickle. When he tries to reach his master to warn him of a dragon attack, he mucks up the spell and ends up seven centuries into the future!

The Practical Princess
Jay Williams

The Practical Princess has the gift of common sense. And when you spend your days tackling dragons and avoiding marriage to unsuitable suitors, common sense definitely comes in useful!